About the Author

Dan Brass currently manages a bookshop in West London. All of the stories he tells are semi-autobiographical.

Rust and Embers

Dan Brass

Rust and Embers

Olympia Publishers
London

www.olympiapublishers.com
OLYMPIA PAPERBACK EDITION

A CIP catalogue record for this title is
available from the British Library.

ISBN: 978-1-80074-604-6

This is a work of fiction.
Names, characters, places and incidents originate from the writer's
imagination. Any resemblance to actual persons, living or dead, is
purely coincidental.

First Published in 2022

Olympia Publishers
Tallis House
2 Tallis Street
London
EC4Y 0AB

Printed in Great Britain

Dedication

To my parents, who made this book happen, and to my sister, who's infinitely wiser than I am.

I

Mrs Oppenheimer's cat had been missing for the past three days, which was concerning as It had been dead for the past four. She had misdiagnosed her companion on several prior occasions, erroneously declaring her feline dead when It was merely asleep or unconscious or lazy. This time around, though, there was no denying the creature's mortality, so she buried It in her garden: less than an inch below the surface of the ground, should she later choose to unearth the animal during one of her occasional existential dilemmas.

(She had chosen to name it It but could not recall why. Perhaps the moniker had stemmed from her unwillingness to discern the creature's gender. Perhaps she had picked the name in honour of her own forgetfulness.)

Mrs Oppenheimer awoke on her kitchen floor with an overwhelming sense of awareness: It was no longer buried in her back garden, despite her best efforts at giving the animal a proper send-off. She did not need to look out of her window for confirmation. She simply knew it to be true.

But where could It be?

She began to systematically search the house, paying close attention to the places where she may have misplaced her cat.

Firstly, she checked her fridge: shelves stacked with poultry but no feline. Her processed turkey slices were beginning to go mouldy.

She made her way to the bathroom to check the bathtub, but It was not there either. Perhaps the creature had been washed

9

down the plughole along with so many spiders.

Finally, she checked inside the washing machine: she was always finding lost items of clothing inside the drum and was hoping that the same was the case with her cat. No sign of It, but she did find an odd sock she had been looking for.

The sun began to set as she searched and re-searched, her body moving in a continuous, frenzied loop.

Firstly, she checked the fridge: no sign of It, but she did find an odd sock she had been looking for.

Next, she made her way to the bathroom. She could not recall why she had come here as she had bathed recently, and she already knew that her processed turkey slices were beginning to go mouldy.

Finally, she checked inside the washing machine, but It was not there either. Perhaps the creature had been washed down the plughole along with so many spiders.

Sock in hand, she made her way over to the fridge to check inside.

Mrs Oppenheimer awoke on her kitchen floor three hours later with a migraine headache and a sneaking suspicion that her cat was missing.

She got to her feet and began to systematically search the house, paying close attention to the places where she might have misplaced the creature.

Mrs Oppenheimer's cat had been missing for the past four days, which was concerning as It had been dead for the past five.

II

As Jack vaulted over the fence into his own back garden, his neighbour's recently deceased cat sandwiched in a less-than-dignified manner between his forearm and his sweat-soaked, inside-out t-shirt, he felt a sense of relief wash over him. He'd started digging in the wrong spot twice. He wasn't worried about getting caught; Mrs Oppenheimer had lost her mind years ago. Even if she were to peek out the window and catch him in the act of exhuming her cadaverous cat, no one would believe her. No, his main concern was that he might not find the animal at all. His neighbour's garden was small, depressingly so, but the night was uncharacteristically dark, and Mrs Oppenheimer had only marked the animal's grave in the most haphazard of manners: two sticks bound together to form a makeshift cross, thrown upon the dry earth in such a way as to provide only the merest of hints at the carcass's location.

Eventually, Jack found what he was looking for. After a sloppy attempt at filling in the second hole he'd erroneously dug, he thrust the spade into the earth in frustration and immediately struck something of a different consistency to the chalky, barren soil which made up most of the neighbourhood's gardens. With this came the unmistakable scrape of metal against bone, a sound which Jack had come to loathe. He'd forced the spade into the earth in too violent a manner, and the carcass may have been damaged.

Jack threw the spade to the ground and, falling to his knees, began to brush the soil aside with his bare hands. Mrs

Oppenheimer had only buried the animal about an inch below the surface of the earth. Within minutes of finding the remains, Jack was able to return to his own property, his prize nestled firmly under one arm. Mrs Oppenheimer would never have to know her cat's ultimate fate.

Jack didn't know all that much about the technicalities of taxidermy. And why should he? He worked in a bookshop, for Christ's sake. As such, Jack had no interest in the art of taxidermy itself: no interest in how the artist would remove the skin from the animal's carcass, using a knife or scalpel to begin the process, but often finishing the job with their own two hands; no interest in how these same two hands (gloved, ideally) would then massage preserving chemicals into the intact skin, now wholly separate from the animal it once sheltered, as a means of initiating the embalming process; no interest in how the artist would then begin to pull the carcass apart with the ultimate aim of removing the skull and, in some cases, the bones from the hind legs from amidst the blood and viscera which were so essential during the animal's life, yet were extraneous to the taxidermy process; no interest in how the carcass would then be manipulated or posed until in a more dignified position before being replicated in clay and plaster, the resulting mould eventually being used to sculpt an accurate fibreglass recreation of the animal; no interest in how, once the animal's skull was placed within the sculpture for added support and realism in terms of shape, the artist would stretch the preserved skin over the fibreglass; no interest in how the animal's teeth were often broken by the artist and reattached so they could be displayed more prominently within the mouth of the finished piece; no interest in how quality glass eyes were sourced as a means of making the animal seem less disinterested in the faux-lifelike position in which it was destined to remain. No, Jack couldn't care less about the process. He was solely interested in the finished product.

Jack was terrified of death. This was why he'd chosen to isolate himself from those around him, and why he had become obsessed with amateur taxidermy. He spent his evenings roaming the near-deserted streets in search of animal carcasses, which he would take home and taxidermize in his slapdash, unprofessional manner. Anything he could do to stave off the appearance of death in the world around him would ultimately allow him to cling to his sanity for a little longer.

Despite striving for lifelike reproductions, his lack of experience often resulted in animals that were deformed beyond recognition. Most recently he had acquired several birds and foxes which, after he felt his work with them was through, stood proud despite their twisted wings, chipped teeth and broken legs. Eventually Jack reached a point where his property was almost completely filled with creatures he had saved from decomposition, but his work was far from over: his attempts at taxidermy were to continue until he achieved his own manufactured immortality. To make space, he began to remove the animals he'd immortalised from his house. He hid them in car parks, derelict buildings, abandoned warehouses: places where the stench of death would disturb only the most troubled soul.

III

Erin was more than just lonely: she was alone. This state of being extended beyond the profound yet temporary loneliness that the average member of the populace felt when dining by themselves and contemplating how inconsequential their impact upon the world was likely to be. No, Erin had gone a step further than the typical loneliness that afflicted the population of the town like a modern plague. She was fundamentally, achingly alone, in the purest sense of the word, and had been ever since her shadow had run away the preceding week.

Erin's shadow had been attempting to abandon her for approximately a week and a half before it finally made good on its threat. It started out with small acts of defiance: Erin would be waiting at a train station or sitting in a coffee shop or lying on a bench and staring up at the sky, but her shadow would not follow her example and remain stationary. Out of the corner of her eye, Erin would occasionally catch her shadow dancing or performing jumping jacks, but it would inevitably stop the moment she attempted to look at it directly and catch it in the act.

These acts of insubordination grew more frequent until, to Erin's utter dismay, her shadow no longer attempted to hide its childish behaviour. As the days rolled on, her shadow grew in confidence: soon it was dancing in front of fellow diners in local restaurants and attempting to stroke strangers' dogs as they walked by in the park. Most people chose to ignore Erin's shadow, in the same way that you would ignore another person's child having a tantrum in a crowded public place. They kept their eyes focused upon their destination and continued to mind their own business; however, it was obvious that they were acutely aware of Erin's misbehaving shadow.

Erin was distraught. Too embarrassed to leave her house, she first eschewed recreational activities, and then stopped showing up to work. It was only when she began to run low on food and toilet paper that she hesitantly decided to head to her local supermarket – a decision that was to have profound consequences.

It was a weekday afternoon, and the shop was mercifully quiet as most of the townsfolk were at work. She quickly made her way around the aisles, filling up her basket as she went, before heading to the checkout: her heart sank as she found herself forced to queue behind a fellow shopper. She kept her eyes fixed upon the automatic doors leading out on to the supermarket's car park, focusing all of her energy upon not glancing down at her shadow.

Her willpower could only last so long: her eyes began to wander from the door to the basket held in her hand, to the floor on which she stood and her shadow upon it, joined to her at the feet. To her relief her shadow seemed to be behaving: it was completely stationary, just as she was. This sense of pride would only last a moment, though. As her eyes began to focus, she realised with a growing sense of horror that her shadow was not mimicking her behaviour: instead of holding on to the shopping basket like she was, her shadow was holding hands with the shadow of the gentleman queuing in front of her.

She stifled a scream, instead letting out an involuntary squeal. This attracted the attention of the man she was queuing behind, who turned to see what the problem was. When she failed to make eye contact with him, he followed her gaze to the floor and saw their two connected shadows.

Terrified, he ran from the supermarket, leaving his newspaper in the hands of the confused cashier. As he did so, his shadow had taken Erin's with it, the two of them skipping hand-in-hand as they went.

Since then, Erin had been alone, but it was not a bad thing. Without her shadow to cause her embarrassment, she was able to go outside whenever she wanted, just like she used to, without fear of having to explain her shadow's actions to others.

Erin was fundamentally, achingly alone, in the purest sense of the word, and had been ever since her shadow had run away the preceding week. She was finally free.

IV

As he sat in the interrogation room, his hands cuffed and his shoulders arched, he began mentally compiling a list of the things he could potentially be kept in custody for. *Breaking and entering?* No. The couple had invited him in. Hell, they'd called him to ask for his help.

"I do apologise for the inconvenience, Father." The sergeant gestured to the handcuffs around Jerry's wrists. "It's just whilst we ascertain the specifics of the situation. I'm hoping you can clear a few things up for us."

Theft? No. Whilst his ultimate goal had been to rob their bungalow, things hadn't exactly worked out as he'd intended.

"Several witnesses spotted you fleeing the scene before the fire department arrived. Can you explain why you were in the couple's home?"

Arson? No. The fire was accidental. He'd lit a few candles and some incense around the bungalow to give the proceedings a more authentic feel, to convince the couple that everything was above board. And sure, he'd had a few drinks before he arrived, but he certainly hadn't meant to burn their home to the ground.

"I do feel mighty troubled by my present circumstance, Father, what with me having put a man of the cloth in cuffs an' all…" The sergeant was starting to visibly sweat. "This just doesn't sit right with me. It'll trouble my conscience for a while, I have no doubt."

Manslaughter? Certainly not. The couple had survived the fire, after all. The last Jerry had heard, they were clinging on to

17

life as the ambulance made its way through the rush hour traffic. "You haven't said a word since I picked you up, Father. Hell, you don't look like you've heard a word I've said." The sergeant, who couldn't have been older than his mid-twenties, was shaking slightly. Perhaps it was fatigue. Perhaps it was nerves. "Are you praying for that elderly couple, Father? I guess I ought not to interrupt you whilst you're praying..."

Impersonating a priest? No. That wasn't a crime, as far as Jerry knew. Besides, he was doing the public a service. He advertised himself as a freelance exorcist in the local newspapers and, for a small fee, he'd show up to gullible people's homes and act to the best of his ability: he'd recite some phoney Latin, splash some 'holy' water around, wave his bible emphatically, the whole shebang. When the performance was over, his client was reassured that their supposedly haunted home was cleansed. He dispensed peace of mind, before leaving with their cash and whatever items of value he could slip into his frock unnoticed.

The sergeant hadn't said a word in several minutes. Having crossed the possibilities off his mental list, Jerry was sure he could talk his way out of police custody with minimal effort. And with no time to lose either, as the priest's frock he'd bought from the local fetish store was making him itch all over.

"Bless you for your patience, sergeant. Let me explain exactly what happened..."

V

Allan awoke to find that the Rubik's cube on his bedside table had been solved. In his mind there were only two possible explanations: either he'd solved it in his sleep or, more likely, he was sharing his house with a poltergeist who liked puzzles. There wasn't much he could do if his house was haunted, as the local exorcist had stopped returning his calls. Apparently Allan's constant need for domestic spiritual cleansing had been keeping the priest away from other clients who didn't stiff him on the bill.

In the absence of outside help, Allan had begun taking steps to prevent any malicious entities from entering his home. He'd turned all of the mirrors around to face the walls so the spirits of the recently departed couldn't find a way in. He'd stitched some verses from the Koran into the underside of his pillow in an attempt at warding off the Popobawa. He slept with prayer beads knotted around his wrists and ankles. In Allan's mind, this was the spiritual equivalent of wearing a condom.

Allan had a recurring dream in which he could only communicate by vomiting up old typewriter keys that he'd previously ingested, before rearranging them to spell out his inner monologue. He had no idea how his dream-self had come to consume an entire alphabet's worth of typewriter keys, as well as all necessary punctuation marks, much less what became of the remains of the typewriter. No therapist he'd seen had been able to make sense of it. His father had always said that life was good if you'd had more sexual partners than you'd seen therapists.

Allan didn't dare admit either number to his father.

He pulled his curtains open and stood by the window, unashamed of his nakedness. Today, he faced the outside world as he always had; with his head in the clouds and his dick in his hand. Allan could see two men sitting next to each other on a bench: one was wearing a tattered suit; the other was evidently homeless. He could also see the faces of the recently deceased drifting along on the breeze.

Allan motioned to brush aside a locust that was crawling on his bare shoulder, only to find that there were no locusts in the room. He was fundamentally, achingly alone. It was like his grandmother often told him in her letters: "You may be alone, but you're never lonely if you think there are bugs crawling on you."

A river ran by his window. It might have been the Thames, but Allan was not sure. His geography had never been particularly good. Besides, he could no longer remember exactly where his house was situated.

He'd reached that special stage in life where the majority of his possessions were held together with duct tape. The crack in the window separating Allan from the river was sealed with the aforementioned duct tape. It was all that prevented the faces of the dead from entering.

Maybe the puzzle-solving poltergeist would visit again tonight.

He pulled the curtains closed and began to wrap the prayer beads around himself. It was time to go back to bed.

VI

72 Ashby Drive.

A well-maintained frontage: a neatly trimmed lawn on either side of the garden path, with rows of petunias framing the grass on three out of the four sides. The homeowner, Daniel Danielewski, a needlessly repetitive name, often received letters addressed in an arching, handwritten scrawl. Not enough people wrote letters by hand these days, but Mr Danielewski was clearly very good at keeping up with his correspondence. A quality letterbox, too – a good twelve inches across, and almost seven centimetres tall. A letterbox like that could handle anything, from magazines to small parcels. It was always a pleasant experience, slipping Mr Danielewski's post through his letterbox.

74 Ashby Drive.

Ms Holly Lynch kept a far plainer garden than Mr Danielewski: it was completely paved and devoid of life, with the exception of four bonsai trees that Ms Lynch kept on either side of her doorstep. She clearly lavished a lot of attention upon them, which explained why the rest of her front garden was kept so bare. Ms Lynch lived alone: her bonsai trees were an outlet for her affections. Each month she received a magazine called *Bonsai Bonanza*. Beyond that, all she received was junk mail and the occasional parcel from the garden centre. She had an acceptable letterbox: another twelve-incher from left to right, although its slimline height meant that Gareth occasionally had to ring the doorbell if delivering a chunkier parcel, and that always had a negative impact upon his routine which would otherwise run like

21

clockwork.

76 Ashby Drive.

Where to begin? The garden was hellishly overgrown, with the ankle-high lawn serving to half-obscure the sinister line-up of garishly coloured plastic gnomes. Their eyes, sitting just above the grass, followed Gareth as he made his way to the front door. He longed for the day when the lawn grew tall enough to hide the gnomes completely but was doubtful that it would happen; as the grass grew taller, the gnomes seemed to grow with it, as if they were bending down and gradually crouching less and less as the grass grew. On some occasions, they would have company: lifeless creatures with cold, unfeeling eyes and disembodied grins would appear alongside the gnomes in the long grass, only to disappear the following day. If Gareth had been able to meet their gaze for long enough, he may have come to the realisation that these creatures had already experienced death. The homeowner, Mr Jack Travers, regularly received parcels boasting a return address that was in a country which Gareth suspected no longer existed. He never dared knock: he'd put the parcel on the doorstep and make his way back to the pavement, his eyes firmly fixed upon his own feet. The less said about Mr Travers's letterbox, the better.

Left around the corner, up the hill, past the bus stop. The number 52 bus was delayed this morning, apparently owing to an earlier fatal collision.

2A Kimber Close.

A far more welcoming house. A simple front garden, with a gravel path and a small driveway; an old Toyota, that most likely hadn't been driven in years, was parked uncomfortably close to the front door. A well-pruned hedge marked out the perimeter. Mrs Oppenheimer lived here, but it was her sister-in-law who was responsible for the house's upkeep these days. The stamp adorning the front of the letter she was about to receive had not been affixed properly: the sender had not licked the reverse of the stamp thoroughly, so the second-class representation of Her Majesty was in danger of peeling off. Gareth eased the tip of his tongue into the gap between the stamp and the envelope and felt the sharp taste of the gum upon his tastebuds. Potato starch, acacia gum and just a hint of polyvinyl alcohol. Delicious. He removed his tongue before gently pressing the raised half of the stamp onto the envelope. Fully affixed. Gareth always went above and beyond the call of duty. Mrs Oppenheimer had an infuriating letterbox: it was less than ten inches wide, and boasted a lid that Gareth had to pull forward in order to push the mail through. It always snapped down as he attempted to remove his fingers. However, Gareth's mind was elsewhere this morning: the taste of the gum upon his tongue had seen to that.

VII

Doctor: Come in, have a seat! You can hang your jacket in the corner. Now, what seems to be the trouble?

Patient: My throat is incredibly sore. I think it might be tonsillitis.

Doctor: Well, let's have a look...

[The patient opens his mouth, and the doctor looks down his throat]

Patient: Well? What's the verdict?

Doctor: I'm afraid it's a little more severe than tonsillitis. You exhibit all the symptoms associated with the early stages of vampirism. That soreness in your throat is a side effect of your fangs coming through.

Patient: I... what? That's ridiculous. It's clearly just my tonsils playing up.

Doctor: With all due respect, I'm the medical professional here.

Patient: I... of course, Doctor. What do you recommend?

[The doctor opens a drawer in his desk, and removes a wooden stake]

Doctor: Now, you may feel a slight sting.

VIII

At 09.34 Billy Haddock had been struck and killed by the number 52 bus, which was somewhat ironic as he had been posing as a dying person for the past two months.

Dearest Sandra, I still think about you every day. I've tried to keep myself together, but the fact is, I've been a wreck ever since you died... Billy was a travelling salesman of sorts. Decked out in his trusty trilby and his nicotine-stained suit, he went from door to door dispensing peace of mind.

My Ellen, my everything, I fear I cannot continue without you. I may soon be keeping you company in the great beyond... "Hello ma'am," Billy's spiel would begin. "This may not be what you want to hear on a Monday morning, but I have less than two months to live."

Dear Grammie, is that you haunting the linen cupboard? I've concluded that it's either you or it's the pipes, but, either way, the sound is pretty disruptive. Would you mind quietening down a little? I'd threaten to call the local exorcist, but I don't think he'd do much good... "Now, I'm not sure if you believe in an afterlife," he'd continue, a well-timed tear beginning a steady descent down his cheek, "but I certainly do. If you have a message you'd like me to pass on to a friend or family member you may have lost recently, I'd be more than happy to do so after I die. For a small fee, of course."

Alex, my love, I still can't believe that my last words to you were "Your cooking is so bad, I think your pet lizard has a better diet than I do." Also, I told you the dog hates me – he's been in a foul mood ever since you passed...

Thus, Billy would travel from door to door on foot whilst the sun was up, and from town to town by bus whilst the sun was down, dispensing peace of mind to everyone he crossed paths with. The further he travelled, the more he gained: a wallet filled with cash and a briefcase filled with sentiments, hastily scrawled on tatty pieces of paper by each grieving customer before Billy moved on to the next house. He made sure to ask for a photo of the deceased as well, under the pretence of recognising them in whatever form of an afterlife the customer subscribed to.

Dad, how did you die? Was it something to do with the local doctor? I always knew he was a fraud...

As Billy lay in the road, the number 52 bus at a standstill nearby, he realised that both his life and his livelihood were being swept away. With his left hand he attempted to slow the bleeding from his chest; with his right, he tried to prevent his briefcase, which had been damaged during the collision, from opening. Ultimately, both efforts were futile: as the blood began to spill out of him in unfathomable quantities, he let both arms go limp and watched as countless letters to the dead and pictures of lost loved ones were scattered upon the wind.

Peter, I hate that you died alone in that awful place. I wasn't there for you then, and now I can never be there for you again...

Billy was not mourned.

IX

There had been an increase in the number of reported cases of children turning into lizards in recent weeks, and it was Philip's fault.

He hadn't intended to create a horde of lizard babies. It was an unfortunate by-product of his poor decision making.

Philip worked for a company which manufactured children's inflatable armbands and rubber rings. They had recently begun to market a new product line aimed at children under the age of five: a range of floatation accessories designed to resemble cartoon frogs. Philip couldn't resist selecting a fittingly named dye in order to colour the inflatables appropriately: *Frogspawn Green*.

He was unaware that most frogspawn was not actually green and, to make matters worse, the name was not the only problem with Philip's choice of dye: it did not blend with the PVC they made their products out of. Rather, it merely stained the armbands and rubber rings a muddy dark green and, after a few uses, the dye would run. Philip had expected the dye to be washed out by whatever body of water the child was swimming in, but that was not the case. Instead, the dye was absorbed by the skin of the child wearing the floatation accessory. It would then, for reasons Philip categorically could not understand, spread out from the point of contact where the dye made entry.

The result? Frog armbands that were as white as ghosts, and children who were as green as lizards. By the time Philip realised that the products behaved in this way, it was too late. Hundreds had been sold. His company would have to do a mass product recall, issue a public apology and, inevitably, fire Philip.

Except, no one realised that it was dye from shoddy armbands and rubber rings that was causing the problem.

Some parents took their children to see the local doctor who, fortunately for Philip, rarely made a correct diagnosis. Others, believing that their five minutes of fame were just around the corner, sought out local journalists in order to see their story in print.

In the weeks that followed, the newspaper headlines had grown increasingly ridiculous: "Lizard Babies Invade Town"; "Could Your Child be Carrying the Lizard Gene?"; "Local Pet Shop Owner Denies Involvement in Lizard Outbreak"; "Local Priest Claims that Fornication and Single Parents are to Blame for Lizard Epidemic".

Amid the hysteria, no one thought to look for a legitimate answer.

Philip did not consider himself a conman, but he intended to do everything within his power to keep his mistake hidden. Although far from a creative individual, he felt a certain sense of pride as a result of what he had inadvertently achieved: he had altered the town in a way that no one else could have quite managed. He had indelibly marked an entire generation and had left his mark upon the town's history in the process.

As he sat at the cramped table in the similarly cramped pub, today's local paper sitting before him in a puddle of warm ale, Philip breathed a sigh of relief. He'd made a mistake. He'd inadvertently created a few hundred lizard babies. Luckily, no one knew that he was to blame.

He glanced down at today's headline and smiled:

"How to Care for Your Lizard Baby: Which Insects are Healthiest to Eat?"

X

She had no idea why the number 52 bus had abruptly stopped in the middle of the road, but she wasn't going to let the opportunity pass her by. She crept behind the vehicle, removed an elongated strip of PVC from her once-garish-but-now-faded pink backpack and stealthily affixed it to the back of the bus.

Jesus is my airbag.

She made her way back onto the pavement and began to walk north, no destination in mind and a sly smile upon her face. Helena had a short attention span, and often felt the need to create her own entertainment. She was currently in the process of affixing embarrassing bumper stickers to local vehicles – a task that should keep her occupied for at least an hour or two.

Honk if you see parts fall off. She was particularly pleased with that one. It adorned the rear of Mrs Oppenheimer's car – a heap of junk that had not left her driveway in years.

Thanks to her juvenile pranks, Helena was no stranger to the law, and so, as she continued down the street, she began mentally compiling a list of all the things she could potentially be taken into custody for. *Vandalism?* Surely not. Sure, she was affixing things to people's cars, but the bumper stickers could be removed without causing any damage. *Breaking and entering?* No. She took a few steps down the occasional driveway in order to reach a vehicle that had caught her eye, but that was no worse than what Gareth, that creep of a postman, did every damn morning. *Causing a public nuisance?* Helena highly doubted it – she was fully convinced that anyone who caught her in the act would see the funny side.

It's as small as you think it is. On the back of someone's pretentious two-seater Porsche.

Her previous prank had nearly resulted in trouble with the law, perhaps because it was more than just a prank: it was revenge. Her last boyfriend had stolen her heart, which was wonderful, but he'd also tried to steal one of her kidneys, which was less than wonderful. In order to achieve some semblance of retribution, she'd attempted to unleash a plague of live locusts in his house.

Pizza delivery boy for life. On the side of someone's moped.

In order to acquire enough live locusts, she had to convince the local pet store owner that she had several hungry pet snakes. Luckily, he was an alcoholic and a liquid bribe was all it took to convince him to part with the insects. The rest was simple: sneak into her ex's house, let her newfound friends loose and get out again. She was trying to achieve something poetic. Something biblical, even. Instead, the locusts had defecated everywhere and chewed through all of the electrical wiring. Which was still a pretty entertaining outcome. Her ex knew she was responsible but had no way of proving it, partly because the pet store owner had little recollection of selling her the locusts in the first place. Thus, Helena was free to continue playing her little pranks around town.

Her last bumper sticker was in the shape of a pig. She affixed it to a police car. Job done.

XI

Agitated and shaking, Morton threw the bottom drawer of his desk open and began to rifle through it frantically. Incomplete paperwork, broken handcuffs... Aha! Vodka! Taking a swig from the bottle, he felt a wave of relief wash over him. All was right with the world once again.

He'd let the priest, the accidental arsonist, go back out into the world with little more than a verbal warning. Anything more than that would have meant more paperwork atop one of the half dozen piles of hastily completed forms precariously stacked to an unsafe height around his office.

He felt the shakes begin to subside as he took another gulp of vodka. Grizzled police sergeants in his position were typically supposed to drink whisky, but he simply couldn't stand the taste. It had been a trying few weeks, and Morton had gradually increased his daily intake of vodka accordingly.

Reporters from the local paper were continually hounding him with questions: could he explain the recent lizard baby epidemic? Why was the local doctor's mortality rate so high? Why were poorly taxidermized animals appearing in the local park on an almost-nightly basis?

He'd thought policing a small town would be easy. Boring, even. How wrong he was.

Most recently, he'd had to apprehend a group of local teenagers who were causing a disturbance outside the town hall. They were dressed as dinosaurs, and they claimed to be attempting to bait an asteroid into hitting the Earth as a means of wiping out their small town. Before Morton could intervene, the dinosaurs began an argument amongst themselves – which quickly escalated into a fistfight – over whether *asteroid* or *meteor* was the more appropriate term for the celestial body they were looking to entice into impact.

Morton sighed and took another swig of vodka. You haven't lived until you've seen a six-foot tyrannosaurus punch a bipedal diplodocus in the face.

Things wouldn't have been so bad if not for his troubles at home. Over the past week or so, Morton's boyfriend had begun exhibiting strange behaviour. He seemed quiet and withdrawn, he'd arrive home later and later each successive evening and, most tellingly, his shadow had begun holding hands with someone else's. The two shadows, his boyfriend's and the unidentified third party's, were inseparable – it was a sure sign that Morton's partner was cheating on him.

Leaning back in his chair, his feet upon his desk, Morton attempted to get some sleep but was immediately interrupted by two swift knocks at the door. "Sergeant?" came the voice of the officer. "I've got someone out here you need to meet."

Morton sighed and took another swig of vodka before grudgingly removing his feet from his desk.

XII

She'd caught her post in her hands before it hit the floor, rebelling against gravity's dominance in her own meagre way. The postman's routine was so predictable that she could pinpoint his arrival to within a couple of minutes, although the neighbourhood pets, both living and dead, occasionally disrupted his timings. *It had been thirty-seven minutes since she ate her breakfast: bran flakes and milk, although she couldn't find a spoon, so she'd had to improvise.*

Holly's monthly reading material had arrived: she tore open the plastic like a starving lioness ripping open a gazelle. She would read this issue of *Bonsai Bonanza* (issue no. 392, November 20--) from cover to cover twice before commencing her annotations, exhaustively noting every cross-reference and contradiction to earlier issues with her red, green and blue biros.

It had been one hundred and seventeen days, nine hours and twelve minutes since she embarked on a one-off sexual liaison with an acquaintance from her addiction support group: she'd been too embarrassed to attend ever since.

Holly Lynch wasn't actually interested in bonsai trees. She was, however, obsessed with *Bonsai Bonanza*. She read it religiously; she could recite entire articles, perhaps even entire issues, by heart. The first floor of her house was a maze of filing cabinets, each safeguarding a portion of her literary collection. They were arranged by date of publication, but her close readings and her annotations made it clear that these magazines were not composed in the order they were published. Far from it, in fact.

33

Holly had come to believe that these magazines were a vast literary saga, composed by an individual or collective of unquestionable, and perhaps ungodly, genius. *Bonsai Bonanza*'s sweeping narrative arcs were bold, complex and subversive in nature, and they hinted at a conspiracy far larger than Holly could yet comprehend. Perhaps this month's issue would enlighten her. *It had been nineteen days, one hour and twelve minutes since she found a small gathering of locusts frolicking in her front garden: she attempted to catch one in a jar, but to no avail.*

So Holly read, and read, and reread, despite the fact that she had no interest in the art of bonsai: no interest in how a tree of choice was sourced from cuttings and layerings – but not seeds – obtained from a parent plant; no interest in how the bonsai artist then maintained control over the tree's growth through leaf trimming and pruning; no interest in how significant outcrops of branch growth, and even portions of the trunk itself, may be removed in order to ensure conformity to the artist's miniature vision; no interest in how copper wire was used, often for years at a time, in order to direct branch growth, thus allowing the artist to tailor the tree's shape to their own specification; no interest in how the leaves of certain species of tree were occasionally removed at the stem, thereby instigating a new growth of healthy – and, crucially, often smaller – leaves; no interest in how bark could be stripped from the trunk and branches as a means of mimicking maturity; no interest in how each bonsai container was designed to limit the length to which the tree's roots could extend as a means of curtailing upward growth; no interest in how gravel, shale and clay pellets were often mixed in to bonsai soil as a means of retaining nutrients whilst also providing support for the roots of the tree; no interest in how anti-fungal pesticides were often diluted before use on a bonsai in order to avoid conflicting with its biological processes. No, Holly couldn't care less about the process. She was solely interested in the magazine.

It has been over two hundred days since it last rained in this barren expanse of a town, not that it needs the extra water: this Other Atlantis has already sunk.

The four bonsai trees on her doorstep were, of course, fake: plastic reproductions to prevent the postman from flagging her subscription to a magazine as subversive as *Bonsai Bonanza* as suspicious.

XIII

When a client came in for a fitting, Dario ensured that he took their measurements down to the millimetre. His hands moved ceaselessly; his eyes calmly followed the numerical markers on his tape measure, which extended and retracted like the tongue of a demented serpent.

He took each new client's measurements multiple times to ensure accuracy. Height, shoulder width, waist circumference, foot size – by the time a fitting was concluded, Dario was intimately aware of the contours and crevices that helped to shape the client's figure.

Dario had been the town's funeral director for a little over a decade, and, as far as he knew, he was the first funeral director in the town's history to fit clients for their coffins whilst they were still alive.

His pre-death coffin fitting service had proven to be remarkably popular; by his own approximations, nearly half the adult population of the town had visited him in order to arrange for a comfortably sized casket.

Once he'd taken a client's measurements, they were free to go about their business whilst he constructed their coffin. In most cases he used pine but would occasionally use oak or birch; he tailored each casket to the client's specifications.

The fact that he had made coffins for such a large number of individuals who were not yet deceased had necessitated the expansion of his premises on several occasions. His small fitting room now backed on to a cavernous custom-built warehouse where the town's coffins were stored and displayed. Some considered this storage space to resemble a kind of deranged museum. In actual fact, it was more akin to a variety of perverse car park: a casket would leave the warehouse when its owner passed on, only to be replaced by a freshly carved one, for a new inhabitant, within a matter of days.

Some of the townsfolk liked to visit Dario's warehouse and browse the coffins. He was happy to allow them to do so provided they left a donation upon arrival. It was not uncommon for an individual to grow jealous of a coffin built for another: "Hey Dario, can you add some solid silver handles to my coffin so it looks more like Ms Selwyn's?" Again, Dario was only too happy to oblige, provided that they paid accordingly.

Far from being a morbid affair, Dario saw his collection of coffins as a celebration of life, with a bustling crowd of townsfolk and tourists alike visiting on a daily basis. The lively atmosphere was taken to new heights by Stanley Sweet, the local street merchant, whose melodious voice could be heard through the windowless walls on certain days of the week as he attempted to sell his wares.

A small percentage of the town's population insisted on trying out their coffin each time they visited, to ensure that they still fit snugly within its confines. Some were afraid that they would experience a mid-life growth spurt; others were, perhaps, worried that their coffin would shrink over time. Dario allowed each client to climb into their own coffin and close the lid upon visiting the warehouse but was insistent that they did not climb inside anyone else's casket. Previously, certain mischievous individuals had attempted to hide in coffins that did not belong to them. However, these shenanigans ceased as swiftly as they began when Dario threatened to install padlocks on the caskets in order to lock the culprits inside.

XIV

Anna Selwyn built houses, but she did not build homes. The various houses built by her construction crew were too architecturally baffling to ever be considered *home*. The myriad prospective buyers around the town were forced into Anna's conceptually confusing buildings for the simple reason that there were no other options available to them.

Anna's buildings were designed to mirror the absurd nature of the world at large. Doors would open to reveal solid brick walls. Toilets were located in kitchens. She'd utilised a pole, of the variety usually found in fire stations, as the sole means of traversing between the two floors of the local police station. Sliding down to the ground floor was fine. However, ascending to the first floor was practically impossible.

Most recently, she'd constructed a house where, in order to reach the first floor, one had to exit into the back garden before climbing a set of metal stairs attached to the rear of the house. Situated at the top of these stairs was a hatch, which happened to be the only entrance to the house's loft. The weary individual, most likely seeking the house's single bedroom, then had to make their way through the loft before taking a small spiral staircase down to the first floor. The whole process had to be repeated in reverse when the house's occupant wanted to return to the ground floor.

Anna's crowning achievement was a series of terraced houses in which the windows, rather than providing a glimpse at the outside world, were incorporated into the wall that connected each house with the adjoining one. As a result, each occupant could see directly into the neighbouring house's lounge and kitchen and connecting hallway. Mercifully, Anna stopped short of providing the bedrooms and bathrooms with these inter-house portals, although this courtesy was undermined by the fact that, in most cases, the shower and toilet were not found in the bathroom in the first place.

Unbeknownst to Anna, her choice to include internal windows had resulted in a bizarre social phenomenon on the small street she'd created. The families who occupied the houses no longer watched television. Instead, they spent hours at a time staring at their neighbours who were seated in the opposite living room, whilst they, themselves, were seated in their own living room. This viewing experience, which some described as akin to watching an elaborate real-time soap opera, was actually more akin to staring at the animals in a zoo or aquarium, safe in the knowledge that the creature being watched is aware of the gawker's unwavering stare, and that the creature has the capacity to stare back should they so desire. Indeed, most families did resolutely stare back at one other. Each evening, for hours at a time, curious mothers and fathers and their equally curious children would settle in on the sofa after a long day in order to stare at their neighbours who, in turn, were staring back at them.

Any sense of awkwardness that this mutual voyeurism may have caused was dispelled by the pane of glass separating the two rooms. The window created a sense of unreality – the tableaux that each individual saw through the glass, which so accurately mirrored their own existence, never quite seemed real. The neighbours that they cheerfully greeted in the driveway each morning as they set off for work or school were not the same people whom they stared at so intently each evening through the glass.

What each family hoped to gain by watching their neighbours' lives with such intensity is unclear. Perhaps they sought tangible evidence to support the feeling of superiority that one sometimes hopes to cultivate in relation to one's peers. If the neighbouring house was in disarray, it clearly hinted at some form of familial problem. Perhaps each family sought exactly the opposite, instead hoping to find proof that the neighbouring household was not so different from their own.

Each household religiously attended to the cleaning of their windows, ritualistically washing and scrubbing their side of the glass in order to show the neighbouring family that they valued their visual connection.

Anna remained unaware of this, as she had begun to plan her transformation of a derelict cinema, the Echoplex, as soon as construction of the houses was complete.

XV

He removed his tattered jacket as he sat down and, once he was seated on the bench, he straightened his tie. The tie's knot was so flimsy that it looked liable to come loose at gravity's most minor of whims.

"Afternoon, Andrew. How're things?"

He made it his goal to sit down and chat with the town's homeless at least twice a week, as much for his own benefit as for theirs. It was cheaper than therapy, after all. He'd spotted Andrew sitting by the river from the window of his office and so, on his lunch break, he went to talk to him.

"Andrew? You okay?"

Andrew wasn't listening. He was staring, mesmerised by the tattered photographs floating on the breeze over the river's surface. Each passing photo provided a glimpse at the face of a recently deceased local resident: frozen in time, but not in place, some fluttered by gently whilst others landed in the river and were taken by the current, moving continuously, as if anxious to make their escape from the area where they had spent their entire lives. Even in death, they found themselves trapped within the confines of the town.

"Well, I'll talk if you won't. I was attacked by a stray cat last night, in my own house. Y'see, I have a bedroom on the ground floor and, instead of having a window in the traditional sense, I have a door that opens on to our back garden. With that in mind, the recent heatwave has left me with two options: either go to bed with the door to the garden closed and risk a sleepless night in the furnace that is my room or go to bed with the door slightly ajar – ventilation – at the risk of exposing my sleeping self to the outside world.

"Last night I gave in. I left the door to my garden ajar, and I actually got some sleep! At least, I did until I awoke at about four a.m. to find that a cat had wandered into my room. This thing was hideous – it was mangy, it had patches of fur missing, and I'm pretty sure it didn't have two full ears. Anyway, I decided to try and scare the creature back out the door, but it was a step ahead of me – as I got out of bed, it launched itself at me and managed to grab hold of my chest hair with its claws. I sleep in my underwear, thus I'd inadvertently left my chest exposed to animal attacks.

"My chest hair, as you know, is sporadic at best, but it somehow managed to latch on to a patch near my left nipple. Next thing I know, the cat's swinging around like Tarzan and screaming like a demon. This, unfortunately, woke my housemates up, all of whom valiantly rushed into my room to see what the problem was.

"They just stared at me, mouths agape.

"At this point I felt my first priority was still the cat, so I grabbed hold of it and, with all the strength I could muster, I pulled it away from my chest. Eventually, I proved victorious and I held the animal above my head in triumph. Y'know, like that scene from the Lion King?

"Anyway, it was at this moment that the elastic in my underwear decided that it had had enough. It gave out and my boxers fell down around my ankles, leaving me exposed in front of my three housemates. I'm not sure if you've ever found yourself accidentally naked before, but my instincts kicked in immediately and I attempted to cover myself with the nearest item to hand.

"Unfortunately, this happened to be the cat which I was still holding aloft. Before I realised what I was doing, I had shielded my bare penis from the startled onlookers by holding the snarling beast a mere inch in front of it.

"I came to my senses a moment later when the cat made a – poorly timed, thankfully – lunge at my genitalia. Anyway, I finally managed to throw the cat out of the door into my garden before turning to face my housemates who, by the way, would not stop screaming.

"I didn't know what to say to them. I just ushered them back to their rooms and spent the rest of the night attempting not to aggravate the scratches on my chest. My housemates and I have yet to talk about what happened."

Andrew, distracted enough by the story to take his eyes off the celluloid apparitions and spectral polaroids that were fluttering past, turned to his suited friend and offered the best advice he could: "None of that would have happened if you'd invested in air conditioning."

XVI

The town's population had swelled rapidly over the past two decades, much to the frustration of Barbara Bartholomew. Her species' proclivity for breeding like rabbits was a worldwide problem, but she couldn't fight the issue on a global scale. Instead, she focused her attention on her fellow townsfolk.

1x pair of forceps, medical grade stainless steel

The alternative community she'd joined three months previously were taking steps of their own. After raising the necessary funds at their upcoming bake sale, they intended to pump LSD and birth control into the water supply. An important step, undoubtedly, but not one that went far enough as far as Barbara was concerned.

1x scalpel, medical grade stainless steel

Barbara had just sent out the last of the packages she had put together. Over the past week, she'd sent one to every adult male in town. There seemed little chance that they would be traced back to her. If any backlash occurred, people would most likely point their accusatory fingers at the town's creep of a postman.

1x disposable kidney bowl, medical grade stainless steel, for the collection of blood and discharge

Would any of the recipients actually go ahead and use the items Barbara had mailed out for their intended purpose? Probably not, but that wasn't the point. The point was to raise awareness, to shine a light on the fact that men were spreading their seed with no thought of the consequences. Ultimately, she sought to highlight an uncomfortable truth.

And finally, the instructions: "Congratulations! You have been selected as the lucky recipient of a free DIY vasectomy kit. Enclosed you will find all the items you need for this (relatively) simple and (hopefully) not-too-messy procedure. This process will allow you to assert your dominance and regain control over your own body, whilst also improving your DIY skills. Before you begin, you'll want to remove your trousers and underwear, and we also recommend playing some soothing music to ensure that you're relaxed. It is also important that you do not seek your wife's permission before going ahead with the procedure. Now that you're ready to begin, proceed to the instructions on the following page..."

Barbara's aim was simple: to set in motion the self-castration of the patriarchy.

XVII

Patient: *A-choo!*

Doctor: ...oh my.

Patient: Sorry, Doc. My allergies have really been acting up lately, although I'm not sure why. I'm allergic to cats – I don't own one, and neither do my neighbours, but something in my house has been setting me off.

Doctor: I see. Can you talk me through your symptoms?

Patient: Well, I've been sneezing constantly, and my eyes won't stop watering. I've been taking over-the-counter antihistamine but was hoping you could prescribe me something a little stronger?

Doctor: And... what's that on your cheek?

Patient: What, this? It's just a birthmark.

Doctor: I fear it's more than just a birthmark. In my professional opinion, you're a witch.

Patient: I'm a... what?

Doctor: A witch. You're in league with the devil – that mark on your cheek is his sign. Your symptoms only serve to confirm my suspicions.

Patient: I could've sworn it was just my allergies. Is there anything I can do?

Doctor: I know just the thing. Step outside with me, I'll douse you with lighter fluid, and then I'll set you alight.

Patient: Well, at least that'll put a stop to my allergies.

XVIII

Grave robbing was still a lucrative business, provided one knew the ins and outs of the industry. Rita had risen through the ranks over the years and, as a result of her seniority, no longer had to get her hands dirty. She donated a small portion of her earnings to the alternative community that had sprung up in the area over the past year, and they, in turn, would visit the local graveyard after dark, shovels in hand, in order to carry out the act itself. Luckily, the caskets made by the local funeral director were of poor quality, making them particularly easy to open once unearthed.

For reasons wholly unknown to Rita, the recently deceased were often buried with their jewellery. Evidently it was important to maintain an image of wealth and status, even in death. These trinkets were never any trouble to sell. The local antiques dealer would buy anything, provided he could then sell it himself under the pretence of it being haunted.

Despite the antiquity associated with grave robbing and body snatching, Rita's business model was a modern one. Gone were the days of unearthing entire cadavers with the intention of selling them to local medical schools as a teaching aid. The market for whole, anonymous corpses had all but dried up.

The real money, instead, came from the bones of celebrities.

This was where Rita's marketing skills had come into play, as no celebrity had ever visited the town, let alone died there. In order to secure a sale, each bone that her employees acquired for her had to have an iconic name attached to it: Elvis Presley's femur; Gabriel Garcia Marquez's tibia; the rib Marilyn Manson had surgically removed as a means of improving his flexibility, thus allowing for a unique means self-gratification. No one could definitively disprove the stories which Rita attached to the bones she sold. Celebrity culture had made grave robbing a lucrative business once again.

Rita sold the majority of her items via adverts in the local paper, although she did allow certain serious collectors to make house calls in order to view an item before a sale. She was not troubled, in any moral sense, by the illicit elements that came with her choice of career. The deceased were of no consequence. Their bones, meanwhile, were being given a new status, far higher than that afforded them in life.

Rita's modern business model was reflected in the physical act of grave robbing itself. Unearthing a corpse here was unlike unearthing a corpse in any other town, for the simple reason that the local graveyard was located on the ground floor of a house on Kimber Close. Anna Selwyn, a local bohemian, was responsible for this architectural quirk: upon discovering that the town's graveyard was located precisely in the path of a row of houses she planned to erect, Anna decided to ignore the problem and build one of the terraced dwellings *around* the graveyard. Far from proving problematic, Rita had benefited greatly from this bizarre circumstance; she quickly came to an agreement with the house's tenants, an elderly couple, who were distraught over the fact that the only house they could afford had several dozen plotted graves in lieu of furniture. Gravestones could be found in every room on the ground floor, jutting violently through the living room's carpet and the kitchen's linoleum and the cloakroom's tiles. The couple resigned themselves to living solely on the first floor of their house where, barring a ceiling fan that was attached to a wall, things were mercifully normal. Upon hearing of Rita's business venture, they were only too happy to provide her with a key to their home, on the condition that she and her grave robbing cohorts would remove the cadavers from their house and nothing else. Thus, a mutually beneficial agreement was made; Rita had easy access to the deceased, whilst the ground floor of the house, which still resembled the set of a low budget horror film, was kept free of the cadavers which had undoubtedly served as a troubling reminder of the elderly couple's own looming mortality. Several times a month, Dario and the team of labourers he had contracted would march into the house, a coffin, no doubt with one of Dario's newly deceased customers inside, precariously balanced on their shoulders. Then, in theory, began the troublesome process of digging a new plot through the house's foundations. In practise, this rarely needed to happen, as Rita's team tended to leave the graves they had unearthed empty. Dario would simply place the new occupant in a vacant plot and replace the headstone before Rita ushered the deceased on to the next stage of their journey.

Recently, Rita had acquired a number of animal bones. The local religious collective had provided her with half a dozen cat skulls, whilst the town's butcher had sold her a cow's spine and ribs at a reasonable price. This was the first time she had attempted to sell bones that were not human – unless one counted the assorted ivory products, back scratchers and ashtrays and the like, that her despicable poacher of a grandfather left her in his will before unceremoniously popping his clogs in a hotel room – but she relished the challenge.

The cat skulls would be an easy sell. Rita's aim was to try and convince the local farmer, who was very protective of the crop circle in his corn field, that the skulls were actually extra-terrestrial in origin.

The story she had concocted in order to sell the cow's spine was far more intricate. Rita's tale began with the elaborate claim that the Loch Ness monster had died back in 1973. In the wake of this tragedy, the Scottish government, which had constantly monitored the creature, then discreetly disposed of the carcass. This was achieved through a covert military operation which had been rehearsed dozens of times prior to the creature's actual demise. In the years since the creature's death, the Scottish government had maintained the illusion that the Loch Ness monster was alive and well, for the simple reason that the Loch's tourism industry would collapse without the creature.

What Rita had in her possession was not a cow's spine at all but a fragment of the Loch Ness monster's vast spinal column, which had been smuggled out of Scotland by a corrupt military official in the mid-1970s.

She knew that it was just a matter of time before some misguided individual bought her story.

Despite feeling a certain sense of pride and motherly love for her outlandish tale, she couldn't help but feel that her clinical depiction of the monster's demise did the creature a disservice. Rita knew that Nessie deserved so much more than a swift military cover up: her mind wandered once again to the joyous, yet perhaps rather cliché, image of hundreds of burly Scottish men – bearded and kilted, naturally – carrying the world's largest coffin upon their shoulders as they solemnly marched through the streets to the sound of a thousand bagpipes, whilst the weeping masses looked on, adoring and inconsolable.

Nessie's coffin would have to be at least thirty feet wide and perhaps one hundred feet long – a task that would tax even the most skilled coffin maker, but which would, in turn, do more for their reputation than an army of high-quality human coffins ever could.

Rita couldn't help but smile as she imagined the creature's gargantuan send-off for the hundredth time. Without realising it, she began singing to herself: "Oh Danny boy..."

XIX

Mr Langford awoke on the floor of his butcher's shop with a migraine headache and a sneaking suspicion that one of his fingers was missing.

A quick visual check confirmed this: of the ten fingers he'd started his day with, just nine-and-a-half remained. Only the bottom half of his left pinkie was reporting for duty.

As he clutched what remained of his pinkie in an attempt to stop the blood-flow, he began retracing his steps in the hope of finding his missing appendage. It couldn't have gone far, and if he could find it then maybe the local doctor could sew it back on. Not that Mr Langford wanted to pay a visit to the doctor – there was no guarantee that he would make it out again.

He must have fainted due to the blood loss. Whilst it was a minor miracle that his shop hadn't been robbed whilst he was unconscious, it was troubling that no one had helped him. Either he'd had no customers during this time, or, more likely, they'd seen he was busy lying in a pool of his own blood and decided to come back later.

Mr Langford found the knife with which he'd caused this messy inconvenience: a seven-and-a-quarter inch blade, two-and-a-half millimetres thick. A quality knife. His finger hadn't stood a chance. This was enough to jog his memory – he'd been slicing turkey! Every Monday afternoon Ms Oppenheimer-Smythe came by to collect three dozen cooked turkey slices for her housebound sister-in-law to feed to her cat. The turkey he sourced was of particularly poor quality, and he was genuinely impressed that even a cat would eat it.

He turned to the counter where he sliced his meats, hoping to find his finger amongst the poultry. To his surprise, the counter was meat-free. In place of the turkey slices was a note: "Dear Mr L, I did not want to disturb you whilst you were sleeping so soundly upon your floor. I've taken the meat slices from the counter – I owe you tuppence. Regards etc, Ms O."

Mr Langford sighed. He was not having the best Monday afternoon. He had lost half a finger, which was now in danger of being fed to a cat.

XX

The Echoplex has been abandoned for the past three months, and I have lived here for the past four.

Its grand opening was supposed to herald a new golden age for our little town: a lavish two-screen cinema, centred around a vast lobby area designed for socialising. In actuality, the Echoplex proved to be a disastrous business venture, not least because of the owner's eccentric taste in films. He refused to screen popular new movies, instead opting for obscure horror and exploitation films that the rest of the world had wilfully chosen to forget decades prior due to their disturbing or insensitive subject matter.

The gargantuan metal angel that stood outside of the cinema, her now-rusted wings casting a long shadow over the building's entrance regardless of the time of day, had not helped to entice customers either.

I moved into the Echoplex approximately a month before its closure. I would wander the streets during the day, before purchasing a ticket to the last showing of the evening. The cinema's staff would go home the moment the last film started, leaving me free to sleep in my seat through the night before sneaking out the following morning. Since the Echoplex closed its doors for the last time, I've moved in permanently.

Despite the fact that the building has stood abandoned for three months, with no one paying the utility bills during that period, the electricity has yet to be cut off. The Echoplex still has running water too. I don't think the suppliers believe that our town actually exists, and to investigate the matter would be too much effort.

I spend my days watching and rewatching the films that the Echoplex was screening during the weeks leading up to its closure – there are just three of them in total. By this point, I've seen them so many times that I can recite most of the lines whilst the film is playing, with my enunciation and timing now matching up perfectly. As I watch, I compose my own film reviews in my head, heaping praise upon the actors, writers and directors responsible for the three low-budget pieces of cinema that now make up my daily routine. I once considered writing these reviews out by hand and sending them to the local paper, but ultimately decided against it. They already have a reviewer.

Wheel Wolf. This one's about a sweet old man in a wheelchair who gets bitten by a werewolf, and thus, once a month, becomes the titular character: a wheelchair-bound werewolf. The plot itself is incredibly insensitive and the special effects are terrible, particularly during the obligatory werewolf transformation scene, but the acting is sincere. Of particular note are cameo appearances by several other ageing horror movie villains, including an elderly sea monster in desperate need of swimming lessons, and a mummy who is continuously having wardrobe malfunctions.

I am the only creature living in the Echoplex, but I am not alone here. Each evening, whilst I am sitting on the roof, poorly taxidermized animals appear in the building's lobby. Birds, cats, foxes, all distorted into caricatures of their former selves; the outside world has rejected them because of their uncanny grins, misshapen heads and twisted wings. I do not know who is responsible for creating these monstrosities. They seek to maintain their anonymity, and I seek to maintain mine. I am grateful, though, as the ever-changing menagerie of deformed animals has proven a comfort during the hours I spend alone between films. Every morning, upon entering the lobby, I find that some of the animals have left, some have changed places or positions, and some new ones have arrived. Mrs Oppenheimer's cat appeared for a single day before disappearing again; I have not seen It since.

Besides the transient animals, the only form of decoration in the lobby is a series of miniature plastic trees: shrunken PVC monstrosities that do a less than passable job of giving the impression of life. There is a name for these miniature man-made trees, but it continues to elude me, despite the fact that I have coexisted with them for the past four months.

Scarecromance. This film, shot in black and white most likely due to a lack of any real budget, is about a man whose soul is forced into the body of a scarecrow as the result of a hastily explained cosmic mishap. The scarecrow, now animated by the man's soul, sets out on a quest to reunite with his former lover, killing all who stand in his way, although no reason is provided as to *why* so many people are standing in his way. The first half of the film is a cacophony of bloody violence, whilst the second half focuses upon the romance between the scarecrow and the only female actor in the film, who seems blissfully unconcerned by the fact that her former boyfriend no longer has a human body. The tonal shift between the two halves of the film is incredibly jarring, but that's precisely what makes it so unique. Apparently there's a sequel, but I've yet to track down a copy and watch it.

There is enough food here to last me a lifetime: sack after sack of yet-to-be-popped popcorn, countless freezers filled with hotdogs, and a seemingly endless supply of sweets, all washed down with copious quantities of cola. As best as I can tell, none of these products will go mouldy in the foreseeable future. I may not be eating healthily, but at least I'm eating.

Night of the Guinea Pigs. A suitably mindless film about a small army of guinea pigs who become both strong and violent due to an experimental drug in the water supply which, for some reason, does not affect humans. The guinea pigs, upon escaping from a pet shop, go on a violent rampage before ultimately seeking revenge upon the owner of the pet shop at the film's climax. The film's frequent bloody violence, perpetrated by adorable guinea pig puppets, makes for a comical juxtaposition, and the acting is brilliantly flamboyant.

A further reason for the cinema's failure can be found in the quality, not just of the films themselves, but of the medium through which the films were shown: the former owner eschewed traditional cinematic projectors and film reels in favour of several old CRT projectors connected to VHS players – pieces of equipment which were outdated well before the cinema was built. The CRT projectors are actually quite good fun to tinker with, especially since I found a copy of an instruction manual gathering dust behind the ice cream freezer.

CRT stands for cathode ray tube, and there are three of them per projector. These cathode ray tubes are essentially glass containers with a vacuum inside; a small armada of electron guns then fire electrons through the glass, thus projecting the image from the connected device into the cathode ray tube... or something along those lines. I don't have much of a fucking clue if I'm honest, this technology is still pretty alien to me. Fittingly, the electron guns, which are colour-specific, each aligned to either red, green or blue, look and sound like something one would expect to find attached to an extra-terrestrial craft. Not that I know all that much about UFOs either.

57

There is an overwhelming amount of fine-tuning to be done on each projector to ensure that each electron gun is precisely aligned to the appropriate cathode ray tube in relation to the lens' magnification. I have yet to master this, meaning that the films are often misaligned and oddly coloured when I play them. This, of course, is made worse by the fact that each CRT projector is connected to a near-prehistoric VHS player, and that the video tapes themselves are clearly bootleg. Each one has the film's title hastily written in a barely legible scrawl across an oddly angled sticker on the tape's surface. More endearing, though, is the fact that someone has taken the time to draw poster art for all three films on each tape's otherwise blank cardboard sleeve. These drawings, lovingly rendered in red, green and blue biros, are of poor quality but clearly demonstrate the passion that the tapes' former owner felt for these films. I often find myself wondering where the cinema's ex-proprietor sourced them from; nowadays my mind tends to wander whilst I'm rewinding the tapes and recalibrating the projectors.

I spend my nights sitting atop the rusted angel, looking down upon the town below. There is always something burning in this town. Alongside the lights from cars and buildings, most of which are extinguished long before midnight, I can see the embers from recent fires flickering by on the breeze. They light the faces of the dead as they drift along together.

XXI

"Some of you are probably aware of this already, but I once accidentally shot David with a crossbow. To explain the events leading up to this moment would take more time than I've been allotted, so I'll just state the following: I only hit him in the ankle, we were only in the hospital for a few hours, and we've since learnt to laugh about it. Anyway, two days later, when the wounds – physical and emotional – were still fresh, Emilie had her revenge when she purposefully hit me with her car. As I stood there on the pavement – that's right, she swerved off the road to hit me – all I could focus on were her eyes. They were positively aglow with passion, with desire – for vengeance, more than anything – and also with love. It was at that precise moment – a second before her vehicle made contact with my soon-to-be-shattered body – that I knew Emilie and David were destined to be together.

"So, ladies and gentlemen, please raise your glasses and join me in toasting the happy couple."

XXII

From a purely linguistic perspective, Andrew considered himself neither "homeless" nor "of no fixed abode" for the simple reasons that the town had become his home and the run-down barn on David's farm had become his fixed, though undeniably rickety, abode. Instead, he chose to label himself as "houseless" – an ambiguous term that could apply to anyone who had yet to successfully navigate their way through a mortgage's labyrinthine intricacies.

He kept his eyes trained straight ahead as he began his descent of Kimber Close, which sloped downwards as it moved away from the town's geographical centre. A number of panicked individuals had gathered in the road a short distance away from the turning into Ashby Drive, and the commotion had caused a not insignificant amount of traffic to stop behind them. The number 52 bus appeared to be the cause of the disruption, but Andrew only registered this out of the corner of his eye, choosing instead to focus upon less trivial matters.

Reeling his imagination in after another of his extended flights of fancy, he returned to his surrounding environment with a single conclusion – one that he had reached many times previously – held within his grasp: he would not want to own a house here anyway, for the simple reason that the majority of the town's dwellings had been designed by Anna Selwyn. He'd probably find himself with a bathtub in the kitchen or a greenhouse in the bedroom or, as was rumoured about the house he was passing at that present moment, a number of gnarled, moss-eaten gravestones protruding through the living room's floor as though they were jagged, partially erupted teeth in a gaping, tongueless mouth.

Ashby Drive bisected the road in front of him, meaning he could either take a left or a right. He turned to the left and began the day's first of what would undoubtedly prove to be dozens of loops around the town.

As best as he could tell, the town had never been accurately mapped. The majority of larger maps either spelled the town's name incorrectly or neglected to report its existence at all, instead depicting an open expanse of fields or an unnamed forest or, in one particularly unsettling case, a red wine stain that the publisher had neglected to remove before printing. "Here be dragons," Andrew mumbled to himself. The one map of the town itself that Andrew had seen, on display in the ramshackle town hall, was warped and distorted beyond belief: roads circled and spiralled off into infinite loops, crossing and recrossing each other in elaborate and disorienting intersections that could never exist in a practical or functional sense. Whilst the map showed some local landmarks, it neglected to pinpoint the location of the town hall in which it was housed, and when Andrew had finally left the building, he found that he did not recognise the road on which he stood.

There were, undeniably, more grandiose buildings than David's ramshackle barn that he could adopt as his own and dwell within – "dwell within" rather than "squat within" as the latter made it sound as though he was assuming a physical position, bent down and primed like a Jack-in-the-box, mentally preparing himself to either perform a star jump or, more vulgarly, relieve himself. The Echoplex was one such example – secluded, comfortable and very much abandoned, on paper it was a veritable mansion as far as a houseless individual was concerned. However, Andrew chose to avoid the cavernous cinema for a handful of reasons: perhaps most practical was the fact that the building was an obvious fire hazard. Taste also played a part, with Andrew finding the Echoplex's metallic guardian angel to be tacky and cheap, even if it wasn't the nightmarish monstrosity that so many of the townsfolk made it out to be.

Finally, there was the fact that the Echoplex was definitely haunted. Whilst no one claimed to have seen a spectre of any kind within the confines of the building, there were persistent rumours and stories told in hushed whispers of how the cinema's equipment would come to life at night; the films left behind when the building was abandoned would play themselves, night after night, to row after row of empty seats.

The rumours of a ghost interested Andrew for the simple fact that they stood as an anomaly when considered against the area's history. Indeed, over the preceding weeks and months and years, Andrew had come to believe that Death Him-or-Herself refused to set foot within the confines of the town. Of course, deaths had occurred within the township's boundaries, but only in the most literal sense. As far as Andrew could tell, a fully-fledged transitional death was a fate reserved for outsiders: those who were merely visiting, tourists and wanderers, alongside those who had physically moved to the area whilst mentally remaining elsewhere. For the majority of the townsfolk, the act of dying was no longer a means of passing from one existence to another; Death Him-or-Herself no longer possessed the ability to shepherd the town's population on to a more grandiose, or at the very least less gloomy, state of being. As far as Andrew was concerned, no one who was truly a part of the town would ever really die. They would cease to live, but they would not pass on. Physical death was not enough to escape the town's confines: this was precisely why the faces of the dead continued to drift on the wind; this was why the town's deceased menagerie of animals was ever present; this was why the embers of the town's torched buildings burned continuously. Any deaths which took place within the town were strictly a biological process. This was precisely why Dario was able to do such good business, but a feeling of stasis remained. Experiencing one's own mortality was not enough to pass through the boundaries of the town and into the outside world.

In lieu of an accurate map, Andrew had chosen to adopt the unofficial mantle of Official Town Cartographer. He wandered the town's roads for hours at a time, attempting to piece together the area's fractured geography in his mind. As best as he could tell, the town was laid out in a pattern that resembled a wheel if viewed from above. The Echoplex was situated at the heart of the town; four roads sloped down from the hill on which it stood, each descending in a different direction, thus quartering their little town. Andrew considered these roads to be the wheel's spokes. Three of these four roads stopped abruptly once one reached the outskirts of the town; the fourth road extended beyond the horizon and provided the town's sole means of entrance or egress. The town's remaining roads each circled the hill in a perfect loop, bisecting the four main dividing roads as they did so. As one descended the hill, the bisecting roads grew longer as the slope's radius increased. However, these roads stretched on endlessly as far as Andrew was concerned, as one could follow them for an infinite amount of time without needing to turn into another street, as if caught in a loop. Now that Andrew thought more closely on the subject, the town's layout was perhaps better described as a large target, rather than a wheel. But a target for what?

The role of Official Town Cartographer was made all the more difficult by the fact that the local geography seemed to shift on a regular basis. These shifts were often subtle and would be imperceptible to a less diligent observer than Andrew – thus, these shifts went unnoticed by the majority of the townsfolk. However, the fact that Andrew was so intimately acquainted with the layout of the town meant that he registered these shifts on a subconscious level: from slight alterations in the gradient of the underlying hill to subtle realignments of the angle at which two roads bisected, the town seemed to remake itself on a weekly, if not a daily, basis.

Kimber Close rose up before him, indicating that he'd completed his first loop of Ashby Drive. His pace steady, he began his second loop of the day, this time walking on the opposite side of the road – a new perspective. Afterwards, he'd descend further down Kimber Close to Jacobi Avenue which he would follow all the way around in a similar fashion, assessing the town's meagre collection of shopping outlets as he went. Gradually, he would make his way to the base of the town, travelling the full length of each looping road at least twice as he went. Not that he could objectively keep track of the number of times he had made his way around these roads – as far as he was concerned, they stretched on without end.

Andrew was never quite alone during his calculated perambulations around the town's conical roads. A quick glance at the pavement directly behind him confirmed the presence of two human disembodied shadows, each walking hand in hand with his own. The younger of these two shadows had joined him within the last few weeks, and undoubtedly belonged to the lonely man who liked to sit by the river and tell funny stories. Andrew had never learned his name. The older shadow was only "older" in the sense that it had kept Andrew company for a considerably longer period of time than the struggling comedian's shadow – for the best part of a six months, as far as he could recall. He did not know who this shadow had once belonged to but did not find that fact concerning: the shadows in this town were fluid and fickle, and it would undoubtedly move to another host before too long. This older shadow had a third disembodied shadow nestled under one arm: that of an inquisitive and energetic cat. Regardless of who their human host might be, Andrew sensed that these two shadows – owner and feline – would never part company.

Andrew felt a great affinity with Death Him-or-Herself, considering how ineffectual the towering spectre of mortality had proven to be within the confines of their little town. Much like death, Andrew's efforts were ultimately unlikely to bear fruit: he would never be able to alter the town, for better or for worse. The people, the animals, the geography, they were all held in a self-perpetuating stasis: buildings ultimately fell, and people and animals died, but no one ever really left. "I am become death," Andrew mumbled to himself. He knew that someone else had uttered that phrase previously, but he could not recall who.

XXIII

Dearest Allan,

I hope that you are well. Your parents have informed me that you're between jobs again. It sounds as though you're struggling to settle into adult life, but I remain optimistic. If you have faith, then the Lord will undoubtedly provide a path for you.

Your parents have mentioned that you no longer attend church with them on Sundays. Perhaps your newfound heathenism is the reason why your life seems so devoid of meaning at present? Have you become an atheist, or are you a member of that new "alternative community" my pastor has warned us of?

My faith has never wavered, and I have never struggled to put food on the table. I also managed to avoid moving back in with my parents at the age of thirty, but I'm confident that with God's help you can get back on your feet. I do wish that you would consider attending church again.

I hope the locusts are treating you well,

Lots of love,

Grandma

P.S. Happy Birthday.

XXIV

I rarely sleep for more than a couple of hours at a time, and I do not sleep every night. Distraction has become my primary goal; distraction from the fact that I do not quite exist in the world through which I glide unnoticed. To that end, the late-night film screenings at the Echoplex have become a necessary pastime of mine.

Insomnia is dissociative. It makes one feel as though all of life's events are occurring just outside of one's plane of existence; they are taking place in another, similar world, which the sufferer witnesses but cannot interact with. As a result, my emotional responses to the world around me are stunted or dulled. This has proven useful considering the horrible things that happen in this town. I watch tragedy unfold night after night, but it does not feel real, so I do not need to mourn or weep. I can continue, unaffected.

I used to be able to see the town hall from the roof of the Echoplex, but I can no longer pinpoint its exact location. I don't know where to look. Perhaps I'm too tired.

The world around me feels fictionalised; hence my need to watch film after film, night after night, in the local cinema. In doing so, I am able to create layers of unreality, fictions within fictions. In many cases, the reassurance that what one is witnessing is not real is proving harder to obtain, considering how many modern films strive for verisimilitude. However, that is not an issue with the kinds of films I watch: unreality is key. They are intangible, wholly separate from the real world.

With each passing night, with each marathon stretch of sleeplessness, my presence within this town fades further. Soon, I will be extinguished completely.

XXV

Mrs Oppenheimer's trusty sidekick, Sock, had recently been promoted from the role of Handheld Accessory to that of Private Investigator. The need for this change was made apparent when Mrs Oppenheimer's sister-in-law and near namesake arrived with a plastic bag filled with turkey slices for It. Upon seeing how much mouldy poultry still occupied the fridge, Ms Oppenheimer-Smythe announced her well-reasoned conclusion: It must have been missing for a long time.

She was right. Mrs Oppenheimer hadn't realised how long she had been searching for her cat prior to her sister-in-law's brief visit. Her lack of progress was undeniable; if she was going to find her misplaced feline, outside help was necessary. Her sister-in-law was out of the question – she had other errands to run. Sock was the next logical option.

Ever since the promotion, Sock had adorned Mrs Oppenheimer's right hand like a glove. She had sewn two buttons onto her new companion in lieu of eyeballs, which had proven to be a laborious and painful process; perhaps she should have removed Sock from her hand before she started sewing.

Sock had already proven itself to be a thorough investigator. Mrs Oppenheimer found herself invigorated, both physically and spiritually, by her new companion's dedication. Most recently, Sock had taken to wandering the house and garden with a slice of processed turkey in its mouth, in the hope of luring the cat out of hiding with a tasty treat.

Of course, Mrs Oppenheimer had a hand in Sock's actions,

in the most literal sense of the word. Sock required that she wander her household, at a pace far slower than she was used to, so that it could undertake its search. The processed turkey in its mouth was, ultimately, clasped tightly in Mrs Oppenheimer's right hand, with Sock itself serving as a comfortable barrier between her skin and the processed meat slice. There was no such barrier between her left hand and the second slice of turkey she had taken to walking around with. This was a backup slice, a replacement in the event of Sock getting hungry and devouring the first slice itself. The emergency meat in Mrs Oppenheimer's uncovered hand did not resemble the turkey slices that Mr Langford normally provided: it was rounded and pinkish in colour and smelled incredibly fresh. Perhaps Mr Langford had changed his supplier. She was not one to judge his skill.

As Sock and Mrs Oppenheimer continued their search, they began to imitate the sounds of a cat in heat. Again, this was done with the aim of luring It back to the house. Of course, Sock could not convincingly make these sounds itself, for the simple reason that it had a slice of processed turkey in its mouth. As such, Mrs Oppenheimer did her best impression of an aroused cat on Sock's behalf:

"Mmmmm-raaaaauuuugggghhh…

"Mmmmm-raaaaauuuugggghhh…

"Mmmmm-raaaaauuuugggghhh…"

XXVI

Jack stared at himself. His misshapen and oddly proportioned doppelgänger did not stare back. This was unsurprising as it currently had no eyes.

He was attempting to sculpt an accurately shaped representation of himself, with the ultimate aim of mounting his own skin over it: with each of his attempts at animal taxidermy having proven to be wildly successful, it made little sense to put off the next phase of his project.

However, creating a frame in his own likeness was proving to be a far lengthier and more complex undertaking than he had anticipated. He allowed himself a significant amount of artistic license whilst taxidermizing animal carcasses, for the simple reason that there was no emotional attachment: he did not know these creatures in life, and therefore felt no obligation to preserve and pose them in a manner which was in any way reflective of their personality. Imperfections were the norm. When it came to constructing his own immortality, though, there was no room for error. Jack's doppelgänger would be his finest creation: himself.

He worked tirelessly, mounting clay upon fibreglass and moulding it to match his contours, but his sculpted self never quite lived up to what he envisioned. He would defiantly alter his sculpture, reshaping entire limbs, only to return it to its previous proportions the following day. It seemed to Jack as though he had been working upon himself for weeks but was still nowhere close to realising his vision: after all, how well does one really know one's own body?

Part of the problem stemmed from the fact that Jack's perception of himself violently shifted with each passing day and hour and minute. He had gifted himself the opportunity to construct his ideal self – muscular, handsome – but did he deserve such a stunning vessel? Jack had been grappling with an escalating crisis of self and was ultimately unsure whether he was better suited to the body of an Adonis or an anthropomorphic mole-rat. At this point in the process, only one thing was certain: his constructed self would either be perfectly beautiful or perfectly repugnant. Blandness was not an option.

Jack knew of no other individual with the ability to control their own reincarnation so precisely. He had afforded himself the unique opportunity to create a new and permanent receptacle, into which to pour his beliefs and ideals and flaws and desires. And even if his soul proved to be beyond salvation or salvage, at least his image would endure. It was unfortunate, Jack felt, that he was trying to complete such a profound task whilst working against a ticking clock: that of his own mortality.

He was struggling to make himself human. The large balls of clay before him were proving inadequate. At this rate, Jack's created self would have rounded limbs and cartoonish features; was destined to resemble a snowman in a skinsuit.

"I wonder how scarecrow manufacturers get such a good likeness," he thought to himself.

He'd start from scratch tomorrow – again.

XXVII

She was twenty-eight, single, lived with her parents, and had been abducted by aliens three times. At least, that's what Sarah's dating ad in the local paper said.

200 grams of plain biscuits, crushed.

She was very nervous about the prospect of baring her soul to a stranger, especially via a mass-printed medium, but her psychiatrist, her psychic and her parents' rabbi all agreed that she needed to be more social.

100 grams of butter and 200 grams of chocolate, melted.

She was already taking steps as a means of reintegrating herself into the community. The new organisation she had joined were having a bake sale on Thursday to raise some much-needed funds ahead of the rapture.

Add some golden syrup and leave to cool.

She knew that her parents would be proud of her, even though she'd chosen her own religious path.

Stir in the biscuits, alongside some dried fruit, nuts and cat's blood. The quantity of these ingredients is really down to taste.

She was making rocky road! She'd never baked before but was sure it was going to be delicious. The recipe was very straightforward.

Put the mixture in a baking tin, and chill for two hours.

She hadn't joined a cult. It was an alternative community. Cults don't have bake sales.

XXVIII

Requiring no time to compose himself, he entered through the revolving glass door of the police station as calmly and assuredly as if he were entering his own home, barring the fact that his home did not have a revolving glass door as its primary means of entrance and egress. A man in a priest's frock, dishevelled and befouled with the stench of smoke, exited via the same revolving door. A faint trail of ash marked each of his steps.

With precisely measured steps he made his way to the front desk and, out of a sense of ritualistic politeness, removed his hat before addressing the young man seated in front of him.

"Good afternoon, sir." His tone remained formal in spite of the fact that the man to whom he was speaking was clearly his junior by a number of years. "I am here to turn myself in. You see, I have committed a number of crimes."

The young officer rose from his seat behind the front desk, a fearful grimace at once punctuating his calm demeanour.

"There's no need for alarm, sir. Quite the opposite, in fact. I am turning myself in peacefully."

The older man's gaze wandered around the room, and he noticed something that broke his concentration for a split second.

"Why do you have a fireman's pole in a police station?"

The officer remained silent.

"No matter. I suppose you're wondering what I am guilty of. Well, consider this my confession. Over the past six months I have been conducting a science experiment, of sorts. My aim was simple: to expose fraudulent fortune tellers who prey on the gullible. The paranormal has become an incredibly lucrative industry in recent decades, in spite of the fact that paranormal practitioners have no respect for scientific rigour. Fortune tellers, psychics, exorcists – showmen and tricksters, all. These conmen and conwomen claim to be selling peace of mind when, in actual fact, they are dealing in deception."

The officer had begun nervously shifting his weight from one foot to the other every five seconds or so, his physical discomfort manifesting itself in the form of a low energy jig.

"In order to expose the perpetrators of these fraudulent endeavours, I took it upon myself to burglarise the home of a fortune teller who makes their living performing extortionately priced psychic readings for the gullible. My reasoning was that, if their abilities were legitimate, they should have known what I was going to do before said burglary took place. Unsurprisingly, though, my first attempt at a criminal act went without a hitch. The supposed psychic failed to predict that a budding master criminal was going to break through their kitchen window and steal their kettle, their toaster and their collection of garishly coloured fridge magnets – depicting a family of gnomes, no less – whilst they slept."

The officer struggled to maintain eye contact for the duration of the confessor's lengthy explanation. His eyes had begun darting around the room, landing anywhere but the older man's face.

"At this point, I felt that my work was done. In my head, I had proven that this supposed fortune teller was a fraud. Unfortunately, the victim of my first attempt at petty larceny failed to report my actions to the police – presumably out of fear that, in doing so, they would expose themselves as a fake. Maintaining their image as a practitioner of the paranormal was more important than attempting to apprehend yours truly."

Increasingly uncomfortable, the officer slipped back into his seat and began absent-mindedly shuffling the paperwork before him as the older gentleman continued his narrative.

"I had inadvertently discovered the perfect crime – no phony psychic would dare report a theft of their property, lest it undermine others' belief in their abilities. So, I travelled to another town and repeated my crime. Almost every town in our fair country has a professional psychic of some variety, you see. I travelled and stole and travelled and stole. It became an obsession, an addiction. To date I have robbed nineteen psychic practitioners, none of whom have reported my actions to the police."

The officer opened his mouth for the first time, revealing his voice to be a rich baritone, far deeper than his small stature seemed to warrant: "Why turn yourself in?"

"I started my little experiment with the aim of righting a wrong: I intended to expose a fraudulent fortune teller who preyed upon the gullible. However, I failed in this endeavour. Due to the lack of attention my crimes have received, I have failed nineteen times over, in fact. Instead of righting a wrong, I merely created further disharmony. Therefore, I am choosing to confess my sins in order to right my own wrongs. I feel that this is the only positive course of action which remains available to me."

The officer rose to his feet once again. "I'll go and get the sergeant."

He stepped out from behind the desk and made his way to a door that was awkwardly obstructed by the fireman's pole. He bounced slightly with every other step.

The officer knocked twice. "Sergeant? I've got someone out here you need to meet."

XXIX

As he sat on the number 52 bus, his fingers dangling like wrinkled, over-moisturised stalactites above his laptop's filth-encrusted keyboard, a single statement repeatedly rose to the surface of Nic Boorman's mind: "It shouldn't be this bloody difficult to get myself fired."

Nic had mentally checked out of his job as critic and reviewer for the local paper about a week after he took up the position which, not coincidentally, was also the same moment he realised that his home town had absolutely nothing worth reviewing. Rather than actively quitting his job, which felt like too much effort, Nic had simply decided to turn in reviews so far removed from what his editor had requested that he would, undoubtedly, be asked to desist from showing up to the workplace. Unfortunately for Nic, his editor had yet to take the hint. Perhaps he hadn't noticed the shocking quality of Nic's work. Perhaps he couldn't be bothered with finding a replacement. Most likely, he was too busy churning out sensationalistic articles on the town's recent lizard baby problem. The term "lizard baby" struck Nic as ridiculous – he, as well as the majority of the townsfolk, had cottoned on to the fact that it was, at worst, a mild skin condition resulting in an off-green rash – but there was no denying that the story sold papers, the resulting town hysteria be damned.

Nic's editor had asked him to review the most recent open mic comedy night held every other Sunday at the town's sole pub, The Arsonist's Arms, which had taken place at eight p.m. the previous evening. At eight p.m. the previous evening, Nic had been in the new sandwich shop across the street, and he had remained there for the next two and a half hours for the simple reason that an open mic comedy night held at a small-town pub sounded absolutely excruciating. He was reviewing his sandwich instead.

Nic's concern with his editor's choice of assignment was heightened by the fact that time's passage was inconsistent within the town. Certain areas experienced a relatively smooth temporal flow, but the local pub was not one of them: within the confines of The Arsonist's Arms, time moved at a pace that could best be described as glacial. Simply put, if Nic had visited the open mic night on the previous evening, he'd most likely still be experiencing it now.

It struck Nic as strange that the town's local watering hole was called The Arsonist's Arms when, in actual fact, there hadn't been a recorded case of deliberate arson in the town's history. Accidental fires, on the other hand, were worryingly common. In just the last week, the fire department had attended two separate incidents: the first in the abandoned cinema, the Echoplex, which had left the town's rusted angel permanently disfigured; the second was started by the local exorcist, who had, no doubt, spent the afternoon in The Arsonist's Arms beforehand. Nic had come up with what he thought was a suitably witty headline regarding the latter inferno ("Arson Parson!") to which his editor had less-than-subtly suggested that he get back to writing his review of the local coffin-maker's newly expanded museum. Ultimately, the review in question, once Nic had made a show of proof reading it for any glaring grammatical errors, consisted of nothing more than a photograph of a goat vomiting. Incidentally, a goat's stomach is comprised of four compartments, and it can take up to fifteen hours for any consumed items to completely pass though the animal's digestive system, making the process of vomiting a particularly strenuous experience for a goat. Nic was not sure how or why he knew this.

The number 52 bus had not moved for the last quarter of an hour; a gaggle of passengers had left the vehicle and had formed a large group around something in the road. Nic was unconcerned. The later he arrived to work, the better, and the longer his commute took, the more time he had to make his latest review as excruciating as he felt his editor deserved.

XXX

Doctor: *muffled, incomprehensible speech*

Patient: I… what… what is that you're wearing?

Doctor: *muffled, incomprehensible speech*

Patient: Is that one of those… those… plague doctor masks? That they wore back in the middle ages?

Doctor: *muffled, incomprehensible speech*

Patient: Where did you get that thing anyway? Did Mr Danielewski sell you that? I'll bet that he told you it's haunted.

Doctor: *muffled, incomprehensible speech*

Patient: Haunted by a thousand restless souls, left disembodied and disoriented since their buboes-riddled former shells were carted off to the mass graves? "Bring out yer dead" and all that?

Doctor: *muffled, incomprehensible speech*

Patient: No, Doc, I'm not going to tell you what's wrong with me. I can see where this is going – you'll tell me that I have the bubonic plague.

Doctor: *muffled, incomprehensible speech*

Patient: Then you'll tell me that my four humours are out of balance, and that I'm experiencing a surplus of black bile. I know a thing or two about Galenic medicine, Doc.

Doctor: *muffled, incomprehensible speech*

Patient: And, let me guess, the only way to ease my suffering is by undergoing a good bloodletting?

Doctor: *muffled, incomprehensible speech*

[The doctor opens a drawer in his desk, and removes a jar of leeches]

Doctor: *muffled, incomprehensible speech*

XXXI

As her post fell through the letterbox and clattered to the floor, she began counting in her head.

Thirty-four seconds.

That was how long it took for the creep of a local postman to reach the end of her street, turn the corner and pass out of sight after delivering her post. She didn't like to collect her post whilst he was still in view, in spite of the fact that there was no way he could see into the shop. There were no windows, after all.

Twenty-three seconds.

She knew that it took him exactly thirty-four seconds to exit her street as, day after day, she had analysed the footage from the security cameras outside of her shop. His pace, his stride, his sense of urgency never wavered. Thirty-four seconds. Every damn day (except for Sundays and bank holidays).

Sixteen seconds.

If he knew she was there, he'd knock on the door and give her his usual speech about the size of her letterbox. She knew most of his rant off by heart ("Less than ten inches across? For shame!") If she refused to answer the door, he would shout through the aforementioned less-than-ten-incher.

Eleven seconds.

It wasn't strange that she had so many working cameras around her shop, as she specialised in home security: she sold security cameras, burglar alarms, reinforced safes. She sold peace of mind, but no one was buying. Business had been slow. Recently the local funeral director had requested a few hundred padlocks but had yet to actually come in and purchase them. Desperate and near-destitute, she'd considered taking Mr Danielewski's advice and pretending that the burglar alarms she sold were haunted in order to boost sales but had ultimately decided against it.

Seven seconds.

Her new business cards would change things though. They were to read as follows:

"I broke into your house during the night, whilst you were asleep. It was a piece of cake. You should consider investing in a more robust home security system!"

Her shop's address and phone number followed.

One second.

Her street deserted once again, she went to check her post. If her business cards had arrived, she would go out that very night and leave them on people's kitchen counters.

XXXII

It is a sad fact that a significant percentage of books, once purchased, are not read. They are, instead, used as an inexpensive means of decoration. A well-stocked bookshelf can give a home a heightened sense of respectability, whilst also bestowing upon the owner of the neglected books an air of intellectual mystique. As the owner of the town's sole bookshop, Sam had decided to take advantage of this occurrence.

Whilst her business was thriving, Sam knew that the majority of the books she sold would not be read, which felt like a considerable blemish upon her integrity as a bookseller. To expose her customers' shady intentions would be to risk her source of income. Instead, she had found a way of having some fun at their expense.

Sam had begun stocking hardback books on obscure, and often very embarrassing, subjects, which she would then hide in phony dust jackets. Her aim was to pass off these literary imposters as works commonly displayed in people's homes, safe in the knowledge that her customers would never check inside the dust jacket and, therefore, never notice the discrepancy.

Her customers, in their ongoing attempt at improving their intellectual standing, were blissfully unaware of the kind of books they were actually stocking their bookshelves with.

Sam's deception meant that the customer who intended to purchase *Crime and Punishment* actually went home with *Ten Easy Ways to Hide a Corpse*.

Great Expectations concealed *Living with Erectile*

Dysfunction.

The Layman's Guide to Home Improvement actually housed *The Layman's Guide to Performing Your Own Vasectomy.*

(Sam had actually had a request for *The Layman's Guide to Performing Your Own Vasectomy* recently – from a female customer, no less – but unfortunately, she could not remember which fake dust jacket she had hidden the book in.)

Sam had intended to hide a large book on taxidermy inside a fake dust jacket for *War and Peace*, but a former employee had stolen all her books on the subject shortly before he disappeared.

To date, no customer had returned to the shop to complain that the wrong book was inside the dust jacket. Instead, Sam's literary imposters adorned the bookshelves of almost every home in town.

XXXIII

Crop farming was still a lucrative business, provided one knew the ins and outs of the industry. Unfortunately, David was incurably ignorant when it came to modern farming practises and, as a result, his barley field had yielded more stress than profit in the years since it had fallen into his possession. Located a short way south of the town, and only associated with it due to the farm's lack of proximity to any other named location, David's barley field grew nothing worth selling. His lack of farming expertise consistently produced a crop so deformed that no local produce wholesalers were interested. Despite this, David felt a sense of purpose in his work; his sheaves stood proud despite their bent stalks, their malformed leaves and their discolouration.

The field showed no sign of ever turning a profit. That is, until the crop circle appeared.

Three vast rings of flattened barley, each of the same size, at least as far as the naked eye could discern. The three rings touched, forming a triangle when viewed from above. The barley in the centre of each ring remained undisturbed.

David was unsure whether the crop circle was created by extra-terrestrials or bored local pranksters. The townsfolk would never suspect that David himself was responsible; his ankle, still tender after an incident involving a crossbow, made such an exertion impossible for him. Moreover, he had no interest in how crop circles were formed: no interest in how the circle artists would select a field that they could enter and exit, unseen, under the cover of night; no interest in how careful measurements of the field's perimeter were taken; no interest in how the circle artists would enter the field through pre-existing pathways in order to avoid leaving their own tracks; no interest in how the field's exact centre was marked; no interest in how precise geometric shapes were then measured and marked out in relation to the field's centre, with rope and surveyor's reel used as a visual aid; no interest in how the circle artists, using $2\Pi R$, were able to calculate the length of the circle's perimeter exactly once the radius had been measured out and marked with rope; no interest in how the circle artists procured good quality wooden planks, which were then anchored to the centre marker with string; no interest in how, after the measuring and mapping was concluded, the barley would finally be flattened with the plank, with the first circle artist pulling the plank behind them over the crops as a means of ensuring that each stalk was flattened in the same direction, and with the same amount of pressure, whilst the second circle artist would follow, exerting their weight upon the plank every couple of steps to ensure that the crops were flattened consistently; no interest in how the circle artists kept the plank tethered to the centre marker and moved around it as a means of producing a perfect circle; no interest in how the rope markers were removed upon completion of the flattening process, before the circle artists made their escape via the same route through which they entered. No, David couldn't care less about the process. He was solely interested in the finished product.

Finally, David's failed crops had been turned into something profitable; the townsfolk and tourists alike would no doubt be willing to pay to see genuine evidence of an alien visitation. The increasing number of green children dwelling within the confines of the town could also work to David's advantage, provided he could convince the local paper that they were actually extra-terrestrial in origin.

David's goal for the remainder of the afternoon was to acquire a number of animal skulls with which to decorate his barley field, again with the aim of passing them off as extra-terrestrial. Luckily, he knew just the person to talk to when it came to procuring bones.

XXXIV

Jerry had already succeeded in wriggling free from the priest's frock before his front door had closed behind him. Now clad in nothing but a pair of boxer shorts, adorned with oddly proportioned cartoon bats, he fell upon the stained and misshapen sofa that served as the living room's principal item of furniture. Even now, soot, ash, and dandruff fell from his hair in equal measure. He closed his eyes and breathed a wearied sigh, all whilst instinctively reaching for the bottle of whiskey nestled safely behind one of the sofa's cushions.

After approximately a minute of his usual meditative ritual – *inhale, swig, exhale, repeat* – he placed the bottle on the floor and, his eyes still closed, reached for a small box tucked neatly beneath the sofa. He slid the box between his legs before scooping it up and placing it upon his lap. With carefully rehearsed movements he removed the item inside: a tape recorder.

He took a longer, pronounced breath before pressing a calloused finger down upon the record button. As the machine spluttered into life, Jerry began to speak in a measured and unhurried manner:

"Gao Xingjian once wrote that 'history is ghosts banging on walls'. Personally, I feel that the opposite is true: ghosts are history banging on walls. By *walls* I suppose I mean our own minds; by *history* I mean our individual stories and experiences; *ghosts*, of course, is meant as a metaphor here – a metaphor for the residual memories of those individual stories and experiences that haunt us perpetually, every day, hour, minute, second.

"We are continually haunted by spectres of our own making. Our past actions and inactions, our mistakes, errors, fuck-ups, do not remain history. They manifest themselves and remould themselves, forever alive and never diminishing; they stay with us, banging on the walls.

"We create our own ghosts.

"This does, of course, apply to society as a whole: entire townships, countries, continents – hell, our entire species – are destined to be haunted by their past. That much is easy to see – our history, hideous and malformed, has been inked indelibly upon the world at large. However, what is perhaps more intriguing is how every individual suffers from their own personal haunting, as unique as their fingerprint, as persistent as their own shadow: a haunting of their own creation, completely unknowable to others. Our history is with us constantly; our past selves are with us always, banging on the walls.

"I have left so many ghosts in my wake. The ones which haunt me are a burden I suffer willingly, but I know that others are tormented by the ghosts of my past as well. If our paths have crossed then I have no doubt that the experience re-emerges on occasion to bang upon the walls of your mind. My mistakes haunt others with the same fevered intensity with which they cling to myself. I can only hope that time will one day exorcise my ghosts from the minds of others."

With a sigh, Jerry clicked the tape recorder off. For the first time in many minutes, he opened his eyes. With practised, economical movements he removed the cassette from the machine before placing the tape alongside the hundreds of others which were stacked dozens high in a chaotic kaleidoscope of a pattern around the room.

XXXV

The brown, foamy liquid spilled tempestuously over the lip of each pint glass and trickled playfully down his fingers as he dropped into the chair. Whilst gracelessly leaning over the table in order to flick several discarded peanuts onto the floor, Gaston began his discourse, which he directed not only to the individual sitting across from him, but to anyone within earshot.

"So, I've been tryin' my 'and at dating recently, but I ain't doin' too well. Take last night, fer example. I was talkin' to this girl what I met through the local paper, an' she was flirtin' back like, an' it all seemed to be progressin' without an 'itch. Then she says to me, she says, 'Just so you know, I'm in a religious group. I hope that's okay wi' you?' So, I, with me gargantuan sense o' humour, I replies back all serious like, 'That's cracking, love. I've been lookin' for a nice religious girlfriend in order to piss off me devoutly Satanist parents'. But she didn't twig I was just playin', like, an' she started lecturin' me on the error of me ways. Somethin' tells me I should steer clear o' religious gals, they're always trouble."

Philip, visibly uncomfortable due to the cramped confines of the pub, raised his eyes from his newspaper and met Gaston's gaze for the first time since he had returned from the bar.

"She chose not to accept your beliefs, even after you'd made a joke about them. You're right to steer clear."

XXXVI

At any given moment, one unfortunate individual holds the dubious honour of being the most hungover person on the planet. At this particular moment in time, that honour fell to Lynd Brunner, who had just awoken on the floor of his pet shop with a pounding headache and a sneaking suspicion that his guinea pigs were missing.

No, not missing. Dead.

Sweaty and disoriented, he rose to his feet, slowly so as to avoid further aggravating the demons screaming in his head. He raised his eyes from his mismatched shoes and methodically began to assess the extent of the damage done to his shop.

The grubby window separating the shop from the passing street had been shattered; the shards of glass were scattered so sporadically that Lynd could not tell whether it had been broken inwards or outwards.

The inside of the shop had received some unwelcome redecorations during the night. Most noticeable was the fact that the walls were now splattered with guinea pig blood. The animals' cages had been ripped open; the bars were bent and protruding like crooked teeth. The guinea pigs themselves were strewn across the floor. Dead. Partially devoured.

Miraculously no other animals were harmed and, with the exception of the window, the damage to the shop itself was superficial. The shop was noticeably bare, but that had been the case for the past several weeks. The cats' cages stood open and empty; that was because a local religious collective had recently bought his entire stock of the creatures. He'd also neglected to restock his supply of locusts after a young woman bought several hundred to feed to her snakes. Strangely, he had never seen her before or since, and he wondered where she normally sourced her insects from. Probably the same place all the local mothers were acquiring locusts to feed to their reptilian children, Lynd thought to himself, a sly smile crossing his cracked lips as he attempted to distract himself from his crippling hangover.

He walked through to the back room and, reaching for a bottle on his desk as he did so, slumped into his desk chair. Whisky. Grizzled pet shop owners were typically supposed to drink vodka, but he simply couldn't stand the taste. A wave of relief washed over him as he took a gulp from the bottle.

He could not remember the previous evening. Was he responsible for the bloody mess, or was an intruder to blame? A burglary gone wrong, perhaps. But how could even the most inept of thieves inadvertently cause the deaths of half a dozen guinea pigs?

As Lynd took another gulp from the bottle, he lamented the fact that he had yet to purchase a working camera from the nearby home security shop. Previously, his sole security measure came in the form of a crossbow he had owned for several years. He could not remember where he had found it and, as of a week ago, he could not remember where he'd put it.

He might never surmise the cause of the animals' deaths; there was no point in dwelling upon the past. Once he'd finished his bottle, he would take the animals to Jack. Jack could fix them. Jack could fix everything.

XXXVII

For as long as anyone in the town could remember, Stanley Sweet would appear at the exit of Dario's coffin museum at quarter past four on certain afternoons before enthusiastically attempting to sell his possessions.

He would emerge at the top of the hill, silhouetted against the darkening afternoon sky with a folding table under his arm and an oversized backpack slung over his shoulder, before descending the gentle slope towards the warehouse. He would set up his table in silence, approximately three feet from the exit of Dario's property, before emptying whichever belongings he'd brought with him from his backpack onto the folding table's battered surface. Then, without warning, and seemingly without needing to take a breath beforehand, he'd let out a bellow that could be heard throughout the town. His sales pitch was simple: he'd shout at the top of his lungs so that the locals knew exactly what he was attempting to sell that particular day.

"Teeth here, get yer teeth here! I got false teeth here, three sets for a fiver!"

No one could predict what Stanley Sweet would be attempting to sell on any given occasion: from old cans of food, with the labels peeled off to add to the mystery, to used bras, which was doubly mysterious considering that Stanley Sweet was unmarried, to pieces of fruit that supposedly resembled celebrities, although only tenuously, to misshapen and rusty wind chimes, which he only attempted to sell on windless days and which he claimed were an excellent means of detecting ghosts.

"Locusts! I got locusts! However, you want 'em – live, frozen, taxidermized! Come get yer locusts, three big'uns for a fiver!"

For several days each week, Stanley Sweet's singsong voice would reverberate throughout the town for exactly three quarters of an hour; at the stroke of five p.m., he would revert to a state of total soundlessness, returning his items to his backpack and folding down his table in silence, before making his way back up the hill.

Stanley Sweet rarely made a sale. Instead, the locals had begun to view his efforts as a variety of street art. Many of the townsfolk timed their visits to Dario's coffin museum in such a way that they might get to view Stanley Sweet's performance as they exited – provided that he made an appearance that day. Try as they might, no one had been able to figure out a pattern to suggest which days he would be setting up his bizarre street stall; the days of the week he chose seemed entirely random. On one occasion, Stanley Sweet did not appear for almost an entire month, prompting mass panic amongst the townsfolk. Rumours of his death swiftly began to circulate, and Dario's coffin museum even remained closed one afternoon as a sign of mourning, only for Stanley Sweet to reappear the following day with his table under his arm and a backpack filled with old VHS tapes on his shoulder.

"Get yer VHS here, the ultimate in modern entertainment! I've got all the cinematic classics: Scarecromance! Wheel Wolf! Scarecromance II! Three tapes for a fiver!"

His performances quickly attracted a cult following, with curious spectators trekking from miles around in the hope that he would appear on that particular day. Despite the crowds that gathered around him, no one ever attempted to follow him as he left at five p.m. in an attempt to ascertain where he lived. He had never been spotted elsewhere around the town; similarly, no one knew where he obtained the items that he was attempting to sell. Nothing was known about Stanley Sweet outside of his public performances, and the townsfolk preferred to keep it that way.

Stanley Sweet's lilting singsong voice, which echoed throughout the town between quarter past four and five p.m. on certain days of the week, became the town's most reliable method of ascertaining the time whilst out and about, ever since the town hall's clock had been melted down for the construction of the angel that stood watch over the Echoplex.

XXXVIII

Each breed of goat digests food in the same way. Much like cattle, the stomach of a goat is divided into four compartments: first is the rumen, which can hold between four and six gallons of consumed foodstuffs, depending on the goat's breed and size; next is the reticulum, which can hold between a quarter and half a gallon of semi-digested foodstuffs; thirdly, the omasum, which is slightly smaller than the reticulum; and finally, the abomasum, which can contain up to a gallon of consumed foodstuffs at any given point. It can take up to fifteen hours for any consumed food to fully pass through a goat's digestive system. In terms of the digestive process, each breed of goat functions in a similar way; how, then, does one tell two different kinds of goat apart?

Helena sat before the now-neglected paddock with her legs crossed, her faded pink backpack still slung over her shoulder and a well-worn book nestled in her lap. She was going to befriend David's goats, but first she had to understand them.

Saanen goats: a large breed, most often farmed for dairy. They can produce up to three gallons of milk per day; however, the yield contains only a small percentage of butterfat, resulting in a cheese that is not particularly rich. Often affectionately referred to as milk queens, *these goats should not be left in strong sunlight for prolonged periods.*

David had bought six goats the previous summer, despite having no expertise with looking after a living creature, let alone half a dozen of them. Initially, he had attempted to take care of them, but had forgotten about them shortly after the crop circle appeared in his field.

Anglo-Nubian goats: another breed often farmed for their dairy; their milk has a much higher fat content than that of the Saanen goat. A versatile animal, these goats can also be farmed for their meat and their hides.

Helena thumbed through the pages, the descriptions of goats flicking past in fast forward. She had acquired the book by chance; entitled *You've Got to be Kidding Me: A Goatherd's Guidebook*, she had found the volume hidden inside the dustjacket of an old edition of *The King in Yellow* at the local bookshop. Clearly Sam had been up to her old tricks again, but Helena did not begrudge her this; the two ladies, whose paths seldom crossed, held each other in high regard due to their shared enthusiasm for intricate pranks.

Boer goats: one of the few breeds farmed specifically for their meat. A mature Boer can reach up to three hundred pounds; they have been known to live for up to twenty years.

The descriptions in the book predominantly pertained to what each animal produced and did not provide much guidance with regard to the physical appearance of each breed of goat. As a result, Helena was having trouble identifying David's creatures. If only she'd found a book with pictures.

Oberhasli goats: a very athletic breed, Oberhasli goats are known for their high energy levels, as well as the sweet milk they produce in quantities of a gallon or more per day. Farmers often remove their horns with a hot iron early in the goat's life.

Helena had begun sneaking on to David's property as a means of avoiding spending time in the town itself. Time did not flow consistently within the confines of the town, so when she spent time there, there was no guarantee *how much* time would need to be spent. An hour's walk could set Helena back by the best part of a day. Time moved less erratically the further she got from the centre of town, and the farm was as far from the centre as she dared go.

Earlier that same day, she'd seen David walking towards his barley field with a wheelbarrow that appeared to be filled with animal skulls. In the weeks since he had ceased tending to his goats, they had consumed everything within the paddock: the grass had been completely eaten away, and the animals had since made an admirable attempt at gnawing through the wooden fence that enclosed them. Closing her book, Helena rose to her feet and attempted to find something more nutritious to feed them with.

"I wonder if they'd eat David's scarecrow," she thought to herself.

XXXIX

Business had been booming at the antiques store ever since the owner, Mr Danielewski, had begun pretending that everything he sold was haunted.

Personally, he was a sceptic as far as the paranormal was concerned. In the supposedly enlightened world in which he lived, he considered it odd that so many people placed so much faith in the supernatural. Furthermore, he found it strange that even though an increasing percentage of the world's population now had access to photographic equipment, not one person had managed to take a wholly convincing photograph of a ghost or Bigfoot or an extra-terrestrial or Nessie.

However, the fact remained: no one bought antiques unless they were haunted. If that fool of a local exorcist had proven anything, it was that big money could be made by exploiting the paranormally inclined. Many real estate agents had reached a similar conclusion in recent years.

So, Mr Danielewski became adept at spinning a yarn in order to secure a sale. The more mundane the item, the taller the tale required to lure in a prospective buyer. Some antiques practically sold themselves: grandfather clocks, music boxes, Victorian dolls. If it looked like a prop from a horror film, Mr Danielewski needn't try particularly hard to convince the customer of the item's supernatural qualities.

The ivory back scratcher he'd sold that morning was a different matter. Mr Danielewski was proud of the story he'd told in order to capture the imagination of the buyer. His protagonist was a cold-hearted poacher whose dreams were haunted by the ever-increasing menagerie of gentle giants whose lives he'd taken with a well-timed shot from his rifle. The dreams were relatively mundane: the tuskless elephants and de-horned rhinoceroses would stand perfectly still, staring at the poacher for an uncomfortably long period of time. He was terrified that they would charge, but they remained completely stationary, with their black, lifeless eyes fixed upon him until he finally awoke in a cold sweat. Eventually, he lost count of the number of animals that stared him down each night as he slept; the herd extended further than his field of vision would allow him to see. Then, finally, after months of having the same dream on a nightly basis, the stampede began.

The maid found the remains of the poacher the following afternoon when she entered his hotel room after he had failed to check out on time. His carcass, still tucked under the bed sheets, had been crushed almost beyond recognition.

As a final punishment, Mr Danielewski concluded, the poacher's spirit had been confined to an item made from the ivory of one of animals he'd killed. Thus, he was doomed to spend the rest of eternity inhabiting a back scratcher.

This story was highly nonsensical, and Mr Danielewski knew it, but it was tricky to claim that an ivory back scratcher was haunted without incorporating a murderous elephant or a vengeful rhinoceros in some capacity. He felt that the dying-in-a-dream element was a nice touch. It had been enough to secure a sale, at least.

Mr Danielewski did not consider himself a conman, nor a particularly talented businessman. Instead, he thought of himself as a storyteller. He took pride in his ability to manipulate the townsfolk through mere words: his tall tales clung to the items he sold so absolutely that he was able to rewrite the town in his own meagre way. As far as Mr Danielewski was concerned, he was a shaman: he was able to manipulate and alter the world around him through his stories and, in his professional opinion, that made him a damn sight more credible than the countless failed or fraudulent occultists whom he was forced to live alongside.

With closing time fast approaching, Mr Danielewski turned his attention to several newly acquired items for which he had yet to concoct a back story: a typewriter which, bizarrely, had no keys, and a book of stamps. It wouldn't take much of a tale to entice their neighbourhood's postman into purchasing the latter.

XL

Doctor: All right, what's the matter with you?

Patient: I'm... I'm a werewolf. Pretty sure I'm a werewolf. Definitely a werewolf.

Doctor: Nonsense. Talk me through what you've been experiencing.

Patient: I black out every time there's a full moon. I wake up, my clothes torn, with no recollection of the previous evening. Yesterday, when I woke up in the pet shop, there were guinea pig carcasses everywhere. I still haven't managed to wash all the rodent blood off myself.

Doctor: Those are common symptoms of intermittent alcoholism.

Patient: No, you don't understand. Afterwards, my skin is all tingly from where the fur came through. I've done some research, there's this disease called clinical lycanthropy...

Doctor: Poppycock. If your skin is itchy, it's probably eczema.

Patient: But, I thought you were the kooky doctor? The one the whole town gossips about? Who believes in the paranormal?

Doctor: I'm prescribing you some cream – apply it twice daily to the areas you find itchiest. Maybe you should consider laying off the booze too, okay?

Patient: Okay, Doc. I'll see you at the next full moon.

XLI

Lemonade or whisky?

I was attacked by a stray cat last night, in my own house. Y'see, I have a bedroom on the ground floor, and instead of having a window in the traditional sense, I have a door that opens on to our back garden...

A glass of each sat before him on the table in the corner of the cramped pub. Each option brought positives and negatives. The choice he made now would determine the nature of his failure as the evening progressed.

...I sleep in my underwear, thus I'd inadvertently left my chest exposed to animal attacks. My chest hair, as you know, is sporadic at best, but it somehow managed to latch on to a patch near my left nipple...

If he opted for lemonade rather than alcohol, then he would undoubtedly be a jittery mess of nerves and anxiety by the time he took to the stage. He would remember his routine but would struggle to articulate the words in any sort of coherent order. In short, he would not be funny.

...eventually, I proved victorious and I held the animal above my head in triumph. Y'know, like that scene from the Lion King?...

If he opted for whisky, then his nerves would not be the problem. The alcohol would provide him with the false sense of confidence required for him to stand in front of a room full of strangers and talk about his life. He was, however, at risk of forgetting some of subtler comedic nuances of his routine and would most likely start to ramble in the lead-up to each punch line. In short, he would not be funny.

...anyway, it was at this moment that the elastic in my underwear decided that it had had enough...

Only one other amateur comedian had shown up to the open mic night at the town's sole pub. His routine, now reaching its crescendo, concerned the perils of zero-gravity masturbation aboard the International Space Station. The pub's patrons, most of whom were alone, did not look up from their drinks. Those who had company made no effort to lower the volume of their conversations.

...I'm not sure if you've ever found yourself accidentally naked before, but my instincts kicked in immediately, and I attempted to cover myself with the nearest item to hand...

He'd spent most of the day going over his routine in his head, ensuring that he had it memorised down to the syllable. It was undoubtedly the funniest routine he'd ever written, especially now that Andrew, one of the town's homeless, had provided him with the perfect punchline: *"None of that would have happened if you'd invested in air conditioning."* This would be the routine that made him famous. He'd be offered countless television opportunities. He could finally escape this town.

...unfortunately, this happened to be the cat which I was still holding aloft...

Of course, his rapid ascent to stardom depended upon several factors, including but not limited to; him actually being able to stand up on stage, rather than leaving the venue due to his crippling anxiety before his performance even began; him actually being able to recite his preprepared routine without stuttering or mumbling or forgetting what he was talking about; and, of course, the audience actually laughing.

...I came to my senses a moment later when the cat made a lunge at my genitalia. No, that's not quite right. *A poorly timed lunge at my genitalia.* That's funnier.

He reached for the glass of whisky and drained it in a single gulp, before making his way to the bar for another.

XLII

Jack continually reassured himself that the reason his clay sculpture was taking so long to finish was because he was aiming for nothing short of perfection. On a subconscious level, though, he knew that there was a simpler reason for his languid pace: he was stalling so as to avoid the next step of the taxidermy process.

Once his clay structure was completed, he would be obliged to mount his own skin over the frame. The logistics of such a gargantuan task were overwhelming, and Jack knew full well that the poor quality medical equipment he had used when taxidermizing animals was not up to the task of assisting with his final creation.

Imagine Jack's elation, then, when a parcel filled with surgical tools arrived in the post one day, addressed to him personally and mailed anonymously: forceps, a scalpel and a kidney bowl, each brand new and crafted from medical grade stainless steel. The town had always been watched by a guardian angel and, clearly, so was Jack.

XLIII

After giving the remaining tarot cards the most cursory of shuffles, he selected one at random.

He drew the Red Pukkase: one of the fifty-eight wrathful deities described in the *Tibetan Book of the Dead*, she was depicted with a set of intestines – not her own – in her right hand. Despite possessing the qualities of a God, she would nibble on the intestines from time to time in order to stave off hunger.

Using liberal amounts of modelling glue, he affixed a green Monopoly hotel to the front of the card. He then stuck the card itself onto the ever-growing mass that covered two thirds of his kitchen table.

Meticulous yet lethargic in equal measure, Ambrose Selwyn took another gulp of cherry cider from the can before setting it alongside the empties at his feet. Disgraced psychics weren't supposed to drink cherry cider. According to his daughter, disgraced psychics weren't supposed to drink at all. Disgraced psychics were meant to focus upon getting their career back on track. Her advice had been duly noted then stubbornly ignored by Ambrose, who felt that alcohol and amateur voodoo were more practical solutions to his problem than positive thinking and elbow grease. Besides, Anna barely came home nowadays, so her advice counted for next to nothing as far as he was concerned.

He opened another can of warm cider before selecting the next card.

He drew Murmus: the fifty-fourth spirit, who took the form of a noble warrior mounted atop a griffin. His role upon the celestial plane was to hold the souls of the recently deceased accountable to any exorcists who may wish to question them.

The card, hastily coated with glue and an unintentional splattering of cider, was added to the slowly expanding structure.

Ambrose had given up tea leaf reading since the burglary. Clearly, predicting the future was not his greatest strength. Instead, his moments of semi-lucidity were now occupied by his half-hearted attempts at *dictating* the future: not just his future, but the future of the entire town.

He'd bought the tarot cards off Stanley Sweet, but had never learnt to read them properly, as the cards in his pack did not seem to correspond to those in a traditional deck. This did not mean that they were without use, though: Ambrose was gluing them together in an attempt at constructing a scale model of the town. More specifically, he was fashioning the cards into a large cone-like structure to serve as the hill on which the town stood. He was using Monopoly pieces to represent the buildings.

This was not the first time he had created their small town; nor would it be the first time he destroyed it. It was, in fact, the nineteenth. The geography of the town shifted slightly with each subsequent creation, and Ambrose unashamedly enjoyed varying the method of destruction. Most recently he had endeavoured to see his little town devoured by locusts, but the insects he procured for the task – from Stanley Sweet, as per usual – were less enthusiastic about the idea than their new owner was. This was only a minor setback, though, as Ambrose had concocted dozens upon dozens of ways of destroying his town, and he intended to try every single one over the coming days and weeks and months. He'd rebuild the town every day if he had to.

Ambrose and Anna, a potentially formidable father and daughter team if only they knew of their mutual passions, would each continue to redesign the town in their own separate ways. Mercifully, their individual efforts rarely conflicted.

He selected the final card from the pack.

He drew the Popobawa: a creature of many talents, the Popobawa possessed the ability to shapeshift, as well as the ability to cause poltergeist-style phenomena and the ability to influence people's voting habits ahead of an election.

A dab of glue later, and his construction was finally complete: he had finished creating his town. All that remained was for Ambrose to set its fate in motion. With calm and measured movements, he doused the town in alcohol before reaching for a box of matches.

XLIV

The Echoplex, the town's least popular purveyor of sleaze and failed social hub, burned to the ground last night. The blaze lasted throughout the night, with the local fire department ultimately proving unable to save the building in spite of their best efforts. The cinema, which closed its doors several months ago due to poor ticket sales, was scheduled to be converted into an off-site extension of the local coffin museum in the near future, under the guidance of local architect Anna Selwyn.

The fire department, who have had a particularly busy week, are currently unsure of what caused the fire in the first place, although a representative has stated that the building still has an electrical supply and that much of the cinema's equipment appears to have remained in use since the building's closure.

Amongst the wreckage, fire fighters found the body of an unidentified young man, as well as the remains of dozens of small animals, all in close proximity to one another.

Whilst the building itself no longer stands, the iconic angel sculpture which stood guard at the entrance to the Echoplex has survived the inferno. The angel, which has proven divisive amongst the townsfolk due to its imposing stature, has sustained relatively little damage; however, some of the aluminium flourishes adorning her facial features have melted away.

Most notably, our guardian angel's benevolent smile has melted into an agonising scream.

XLV

Mrs Oppenheimer and Sock stood over the oft-disturbed soil. Together, they grasped a single shovel. The act of digging had proven laborious in spite of the hole's shallow depth; Sock was panting silently, failing to catch a breath in spite of Mrs Oppenheimer's efforts at synchronising Sock's gasps with her own laboured breathing.

It had finally returned home, and Mrs Oppenheimer was preparing to bury her cadaverous cat for a second time.

It was definitely It, although the animal's proportions had contorted considerably since the first burial. It's left legs, both front and back, were noticeably shorter than the right pair, and the creature's eyes were now two different colours: the left a vivid pink, the right a shade of green that could only be described as frogspawn. Mrs Oppenheimer could not recall which of these violently opposed hues her feline's eyes had been prior to death, but she was sure that the two eyes had at least been the same colour in life.

The animal's coat was covered with a fine layer of ash and extinguished embers.

As best as she could tell, though, her deceased cat seemed both happy and healthy. Wherever the animal had been, It had returned home smiling.

Her neighbour, Jack, was standing at his window in order to view the grand send-off. He had remained in the same spot, completely unmoving, for the past few hours – Jack had clearly been anticipating It's second burial for quite some time. Both Mrs

Oppenheimer and Sock were touched to know that their neighbour cared so deeply about the fate of an animal he hardly knew.

After a moment of silence, and under the glassy, unwavering stare of her neighbour, she buried her cat for the second time.

Mrs Oppenheimer's cat had been dead for the past eight days; It had spent the past seven saying farewell to the town.

Printed in Great Britain
by Amazon

16227304R00068